The characters and events portrayed in this book are fictitious. Any similarity to real persons, living or dead, is coincidental and not intended by the author. Any reference to real locations is only for atmospheric effect, and in no way truly represents those locations.

Copyright © 2021 by Ryan Casey

Cover design by Miblart

All rights reserved.

No part of this book may be reproduced in any form or by any electronic or mechanical means, including information storage and retrieval systems, without written permission from the author, except for the use of brief quotations in a book review.

Published by Higher Bank Books

SURVIVE THE DARKNESS

A Post Apocalyptic EMP Survival Thriller

RYAN CASEY

GET A POST APOCALYPTIC NOVEL FOR FREE

To instantly receive an exclusive post apocalyptic novel totally free, sign up for Ryan Casey's author newsletter at: ryancaseybooks.com/fanclub

CHAPTER ONE

Cameron Baker clutched onto the arms of his seat and prayed this flight would end as soon as bloody possible.

He hated flying. Hated everything about it. He hated the pressure in his skull as the plane hurtled through the sky. He hated the false pretence of kindness from the air hostesses, those big plastic smiles and unnaturally wide blue eyes staring down at him. And he hated the sound of the engine, whirring away in the background, that constant drone drowning out anything he was trying to listen to.

And the way people flicked through magazines and kids played on iPads like being thirty thousand feet in the air was the most normal situation to be in.

But more than anything, Cameron Baker hated flying because he was scared.

He didn't like admitting it, this fear. He knew it was a pretty common phobia. One of the biggest phobias, apparently. But he didn't like anything that tarnished his macho image. He worked in the building trade, which wasn't exactly the most sensitive industry.

And it wasn't like he really fit in as a builder in the first place, in all honesty. He wasn't exactly the typical builder bloke. He was pretty long-limbed and gangly. Daz and Harry always called him Heroin Harry, even though he wasn't called Harry at all, something a few of the other lads on site didn't seem to realise. And he was quieter than the bulk of them, too. Didn't like to chat about women or "birds" as they called them. Not interested in drinking heavily or partying, or doing drugs. Never the life for him.

He just wanted to go to work, get paid, and go back home to Melissa and Noah for a quiet life.

Sometimes, people told him he was an underachiever. Particularly his dad. He'd done pretty well at school and could have gone to university if he'd really wanted to. Become a doctor.

But instead, he just wanted to get earning young. Ironically, it was the pressure from the very same dad which pushed him in that direction. *Get earning young, get some money in the bank, and get yourself on the housing ladder, boy.*

He smiled when he thought of his old dad. His old dad, now living in sheltered housing, married three times and rinsed out of his finances every single time.

How did getting earning young and getting money in the bank work for you, Dad?

Bet you wish I'd become a doctor now, don't you?

But even so, Cameron was happy with a quiet life. He was in his early thirties, and he'd been single for quite some time.

That's until he met Melissa three years ago.

He liked being single. He enjoyed his alone time. Liked getting in from work, cooking himself a microwave meal, and sitting back on his PlayStation for a few hours. He was an introvert, so that life didn't bother him. In fact, it suited him to a tee.

But when Melissa came along, everything changed.

Especially because Melissa had a little boy, Noah.

He looked at the seat beside him. Saw Noah sitting there, hands on his lap. Saw his brown hair and blue eyes. His Manchester United T-shirt with Rashford on the back. He could hear the whirring of the engine. Every little shift in its noises made him jump and look around to gauge the panic on the faces of the cabin crew. Every beep or buzz or seatbelt alarm had him convinced the end was nigh. He couldn't help it. It was his fear. Everyone had fears.

"You okay, honey?"

He looked up past Noah, and he saw Melissa.

She had gorgeous, piercing blue eyes. Curly brown hair. And a smile to die for.

She was such a nice person. So good. So pure. Ever since meeting her at the Flash bar that night in November when he was out with his friends, he'd been drawn to her immediately. Always thought love at first sight was nonsense, but since meeting Melissa, yeah, he was a convert.

The first three months of dating had been a little on and off. Mostly due to his commitment issues. Didn't help that the lads at work got wind of it and started trying to track down her Facebook to tell her how much "Horny Heroin Harry wants 2 do u".

But three years ago, Melissa changed everything. And they were together, properly together. Together, engaged, and he was pretty much a dad to Noah.

"Noah or me?" Cameron asked.

Melissa rolled her eyes. "You."

Cameron nodded. He didn't want to let Noah think he was some kind of weakling in front of him. Not when he was supposed to be a provider. A caregiver. Noah's biological father wasn't worth jack shit and contributed nothing, so Cameron didn't want this kid growing up thinking all men were just useless.

He needed a father figure in his life. A strong male influence to counteract the amazing mother alongside him on this journey.

But he found it hard not to be edgy right now.

Especially with the dreams he'd been having.

They were off on holiday. First time out of the country for Cameron since he was a kid, which he fully realised was a bit weird. Mostly due to his fear of flying. But it wasn't unfounded. He'd perforated an eardrum in nasty turbulence on the way back from Spain when he was little. Remembered the agony to this day. Swore never to fly again.

But here he was. All in the name of family.

Truth be told, he was excited. Excited to get to Turkey and get away, especially after all the corona crap last year, and especially at New Year. Although they'd cocked up a little bit with the flights and were actually heading back just as the New Year broke in Dalaman.

As for corona… that bought him a bit of time and a few excuses not to go abroad, but everyone had been vaccinated now, and another strain hadn't run rampant, so life was pretty much returning back to something like normal—with the odd exception of more regular mask-wearing and a few local lockdowns in spike areas.

But the world was pretty much back to normal. And that meant he couldn't hide from his sense of duty to his family. Melissa's desire to take her seven-year-old boy abroad somewhere, for the first time.

He tried to bargain at first. Tried to persuade her to just go to France. They could get the ferry over, then drive down to Paris. Take Noah to Disneyland.

But Melissa told him she really wanted to go to a beach somewhere and someplace still warm over winter. And that flying was the best way.

And in the end, it became clear Cameron couldn't hide behind his phobia much longer.

"You'll be okay," Melissa mouthed. They were an hour into the flight, and Cameron was pretty on edge. Not as nervous as before, admittedly, but still not entirely comfortable, either.

But he just kept taking deep breaths.

Just telling himself, repeatedly, that everything was going to be okay.

That they were an hour in and hadn't had a problem so far.

Everything was going to be—

A bang.

The plane rattled.

He hovered off his seat, just for a second.

And for a moment, he swore he heard a scream and swore it was himself.

He looked around, heart racing.

Saw Noah staring up at him. Wide-eyed. Fearful.

And as terrified as Cameron was, he didn't want to show Noah that was the case.

He didn't want Noah to grow up fearful.

He wanted to be a father figure.

Wanted to protect him.

Melissa looked over at Cameron, a glimmer of concern on her face for the pair of them. Somewhere across the cabin, a woman screamed, which wasn't helping with the mood here.

But Cameron just had to keep his cool.

Keep things calm.

Be a father.

"Hey," he said.

Noah looked around. His big blue eyes were bloodshot and tearful. He stared at Noah with horror, with fear.

"It's okay," Cameron said. His own hands shaking but trying not to show that was the case. "It's—it's just turbulence. It happens all the time."

"But I'm scared."

"I know. I... I used to be scared of planes too, you know? But you know what always helps me?"

"What?"

"Count back from one hundred. See if you're still worried when you get to one. Okay?"

Noah narrowed his eyes. Looked unsure.

"Go on," Cameron said. "Give it a try and see how it works."

Noah nodded. Then silently, he started to whisper the numbers, count his way down.

And as Cameron sat there, he realised Noah was holding his hand.

And he realised he was counting, too.

He realised he wasn't afraid.

He looked over Noah at Melissa, who Noah sat between.

Saw the smile stretch across her face.

"Thank you," she said. "I'm so proud. I'm so—"

A bang.

All the lights went out.

Only this time, they didn't come back on.

And this time, it wasn't long before Cameron was screaming.

It would be the last sound he ever made.

But the last sound he ever heard?

Little Noah counting down from one hundred, as the plane hurtled towards the earth, in total darkness.

CHAPTER TWO

New Year's Eve
20:00
Four Hours Before the Event...

* * *

Max stared into the mirror and really, really wished he didn't have to work tonight.

It was eight p.m., New Year's Eve. He could already hear the fireworks starting in the distance outside. His home was peaceful. Well out of the way of any riff-raff. Only a couple of houses up here in the middle of nowhere, right on the edge of the Beacon Fell country park and nature reserve, and he didn't really know much about his neighbours. Everyone up here preferred to keep themselves to themselves. Max liked it that way, too. Suited him perfectly. Far preferred the rural lifestyle. Trees. Fields. Nobody to worry about for miles.

And sure. They'd built a little community estate at the foot of the hill a few years back, which housed some less than savoury types. But they didn't bother him. As long as they kept out of his way, all was good.

He could hear the rain outside. Part of him hoped that meant tonight would be a quieter one, but who was he kidding? It was New Year's Eve for a start, which was always a shitshow. And it was the first New Year's Eve since the whole coronavirus pandemic crippled the globe. First real chance for a party, restriction-free.

Make no mistake about it, tonight was going to be an absolute blowout, and he hated the thought.

He stared into the mirror. Looked older and more miserable every time he caught his reflection. He was in his forties. Well built. Looked after himself pretty well. None of those designer gyms you see fancy pricks going to. He didn't have time for that calorie-counting, protein-weighing bullshit. Just proper stuff. His own sets of weights. Lift until he was knackered, run the next day, and then back to the lifting the day after.

People were so obsessed with process these days. They forgot we all come from ancestors who didn't have the luxury of MyFitness apps or whatever the hell these rip-off subscriptions were.

We came from a breed of people who got fit because they *had* to be fit. Not because they wanted to look good on a damned Tinder profile picture.

His beard looked a little long and needed a trim. He smirked a bit when he saw a grey hair there. Remembered Kathryn pointing out his first grey beard hair all those years ago. How he swore he'd find a grey hair on her head too to make up for it. Pretending he'd found one, even though he was blatantly lying.

"Haven't done too bad on the greying front, eh?" he muttered.

Nobody responded.

As always, nobody responded.

His smile dropped a little as he looked at his dark hair. As he buttoned up his black shirt, a little too tight for his body. And as he grabbed his fleece and zipped it right up. He stood there. Took a few deep breaths. Really grounded himself in the moment.

Tonight was going to be a shitshow. Drunken people were the worst. Drunken people on New Year's Eve were even worse. And drunken people on New Year's Eve right at the end of a global pandemic were the *absolute* worst.

He hated people. Make no mistake about that. If he had it his way, he'd never have to deal with another single bloody person again in his life.

But at least on this job, he didn't *have* to like people. He didn't have to get on with people, not as a security guard. Sure, in the army, he'd had to cooperate with people. And in his years as a police officer, he'd had to get on with people, too. Can't get away with being a dick all the time. You could try, of course. He knew a bloke called Detective Brian McDone once. He was pretty old school. What you see is what you get, for better or for worse.

But look what happened to him. He ended up buggering off to Spain on early retirement because he couldn't hack it anymore.

Last Max heard, he'd broken his ankle in a jet ski accident.

He looked around at the double bed. One side slightly more sunken than the other, the side he always slept on. He looked at the room, dusty and dark. A few cobwebs hanging down from the wooden beams of the cottage above. Clothes scattered around the floor. A few coffee cups on the side of the bedside table, and a couple of half-emptied beer glasses, too.

It wasn't too bad. Sure, Kathryn wouldn't have liked it. She was always so house-proud. But he didn't have anyone coming round here these days. Didn't have any guests to worry about.

And he liked it that way.

So if he wasn't trying to impress anyone, what was he worrying about, really?

He went to grab his phone off the bed when he heard something fall across the room.

He looked back, over towards the mirror he'd just been staring into, all murky and smudged.

Beside it, the photograph lying face down.

He felt a knot in his stomach. He didn't really want to go over there. Didn't really want to see. Because it just brought it all back. Reminded him of what he'd had.

Of what he'd lost.

But he walked over. Slowly.

Heart racing.

And when he reached it, he stopped.

Took a few breaths.

Then he lifted it.

He saw the photograph right away, and he was back there again.

The beach. Greece, five years ago. Stiflingly hot summer. Really bloody warm.

Him.

Kathryn.

And little David, too.

He looked at the three of them in that photo, and he could hear the crashing of the waves, the kids' laughter. He could smell the salt of the sea and the sun cream in the air. He could feel the warmth of the sun on his skin.

And he could feel happiness.

A feeling that didn't seem to align with him anymore.

An item of clothing that didn't fit.

That'd shrunk in the wash.

He swallowed a lump in his throat.

And he turned the photo around.

He wasn't sure he wanted to look at it again when he got back tonight.

Wasn't sure he wanted to see.

He stood there a few seconds as his heart started racing, beating, thumping.

The memory.
The shouts.
The screams.
He closed his eyes.
Shook his head.
No.

And then he took a deep breath, opened his eyes, and he was back in the bedroom again.

He didn't have to go there. He didn't have to visit the past again. Not tonight.

He went to grab his keys from the bedside cabinet when he saw his lights flicker, just for a moment.

But Max thought nothing of it at the time.

Nobody did.

CHAPTER THREE

New Year's Eve
21:00
Three Hours Before the Event...

* * *

Aofie went to hit "send" on her university application when she realised there was an entire other page to fill in.

No rest for the wicked.

It was late. She only knew that because it was dark outside. The last time she'd left the room, it was light. Or had she been out since to grab a glass of water? She wasn't sure, only that her eyes were red and sore, and she had a nasty headache.

But she really needed to get this application done. She really needed to get her life back in order.

And if that meant sacrificing the whole day and dedicating it to applying for as many university courses in zoology as she possibly could, then that's absolutely what she would do.

She could hear laughter outside. Heard something smashing

and a chorus of "whoas." It sounded busy out there. Busier than usual. She didn't exactly live in the nicest part of Preston. Outside the middle of the city centre, but in a really dodgy area. The kind of area she didn't like walking through to the city, so always took a bus, even though it wasn't an incredibly long stretch.

And sure, Preston wasn't bad as far as cities went in terms of crime. There were no big gangs that she knew of. Didn't seem to suffer the same drug and homelessness issues as other major cities, even though she did see the odd rough sleeper. It was almost as if even the criminals themselves knew it was a bit shitty, really. Like, there wasn't a whole lot to do here. She'd always dreamed of moving out and away to a big city, to a metropolis, where everything was on her doorstep.

And then she'd met Jason, and everything changed.

A bitter taste in her mouth.

A tightness and a cramping right in her gut.

Best not to think of him. Thinking about the past will do you no good.

She looked around her room. It was all pretty minimalistic. No pictures on the walls. The double bed didn't even have a quilt cover. Everything was all so neat and tidy, but it was that way because there was barely anything in here.

There was a real sense of impermanence about the place. For Aoife, it was as if by not decorating the room and not doing it up, she was maintaining the illusion in her mind that she wasn't here to stay.

But she'd lived here for eighteen months now, and it didn't feel like anything was changing.

She leaned back and stretched out. Let out a yawn. She was getting a whole lot more tired a whole lot earlier these days. She was thirty-three, so she was hardly old. But definitely too old to be living in a flat share with three younger women. And definitely too old to be applying for a university course for a radical change in career.

She thought about her life before. Jason. The pregnancy. The wedding. How perfect everything seemed.

And she thought about how much everything fell apart. How quickly it fell apart.

The marriage.

Her career.

Everything.

She took a deep breath.

Swallowed a lump in her throat.

Best not to think about that.

Best to keep that where it belonged.

She dragged herself across the wooden flooring on her wheeled office chair when she heard three bangs at her door.

"Aoife? You ready yet?"

You ready yet? What was that supposed to mean? Was she supposed to be ready for something?

"I... Um—"

"We're gonna start drinking soon." It was Kayleigh. Clearly Kayleigh. She could always tell from the squeakiness of her voice. "You'd better be ready, darl. It's New Year's Eve, after all."

New Year's Eve.

Shit.

Shit, shit, shit.

How could she forget? She'd been so caught up in applying for all the zoology courses she could that she'd totally forgotten it was New Year's Eve.

And even worse, she'd made a vague promise a few weeks ago to go out with "the girls" tonight.

"I... I'm not feeling too well," Aoife said.

"What? Rubbish. That's your classic excuse."

"I don't make excuses."

"You promised you'd come out, Aoife," Kayleigh shouted through the door. A slight hint of annoyance in her voice. "After everything going on with me and Daniel lately, I thought... I just thought maybe you'd come for a few drinks with us to help forget everything. They're switching the lights on at midnight. There's a band playing and everything. It's gonna be ace!"

Aoife envied Kayleigh's somewhat youthful enthusiasm. But she found it hard to muster up any sort of enthusiasm when it came to a Preston lights switch on or a vague band who'd actually agree to play the switch on around here when there were no doubt far more attractive options available.

"I—I don't remember promising anything," Aoife said.

"For God's sakes," Kayleigh said with a sigh. Aoife could tell she was pissed off now. "You're always the same. Too bloody stubborn and too bloody independent for your own good. Like you're better than us."

Aoife opened her mouth to respond. But she knew how arguing back to an accusation of being stubborn would make her look.

She felt a little hurt by that. Was that how they saw her? Aloof? Of course, she was a bit more world-wise than these girls. She'd been a solicitor before her life went awry, after all. Before she moved here seeking a fresh start after the job just got too much for her.

But she was always pleasant with the girls. Always tried her best.

But shit. Now she thought about it... *had* she been a little distant? A little aloof?

"Forget it," Kayleigh said. "Enjoy your night. I'll make sure we enjoy ours—"

"I'll come," Aoife said.

A pause.

"What?"

"I said I'll come. Give me a chance to get ready, and I'll come. The lights. They'll be... they'll be fun."

Another pause. Longer, this time.

Then a laugh.

"Great. That's great, Aoife. Be ready in an hour. It's about time we got you royally wasted."

She ran off down the corridor, towards the kitchen, towards the music, towards the laughter of the other girls.

Aoife turned around to her MacBook. To that full page remaining of her current application.

"Screw it," she said.

She saved her progress, then she closed the tab, and then shut the lid of the MacBook before climbing off her chair and walking over to her wardrobe.

She didn't see the news of inexplicable solar activity and bizarre electrical phenomena across the globe open in her other tab...

CHAPTER FOUR

New Year's Eve
22:00
Two Hours Before the Event...

* * *

"ID, please?"

The scrawny little kid stared up at Max, and his eyes widened right away. Immediate enough for Max to know there's no way this guy was eighteen and absolutely no way he was getting in this nightclub tonight.

But he dug his hands into his wallet for it anyway. Scrambled around for it. "I—I think it's in here somewhere."

Max stood there and smirked. He'd let the kid search for this ID Max knew already definitely didn't exist. One way of making his night as a security guard go a little easier, on the doors of the Lava nightclub in the middle of the city centre. It was only ten o clock, but everyone was already packing into here for drinks before spilling onto the streets for the big light switch on at midnight.

"Come on, prick!" someone shouted from behind, urging the lad on in his search for ID.

"Yeah, four-eyes," another of the thugs called. "Freezing my arse off out here!"

Max saw the kid look up at him, wide-eyed behind those glasses of his, and the look of regret on his face.

"Go on," Max said. "In you go."

The lad's jaw dropped. "I—"

"Don't talk yourself out of it. In there. Now. Before I change my mind."

The lad nodded, scuttled past, clearly not believing his luck.

But hell. As far as Max saw it, a nightclub on New Year's Eve was a special kind of torture. The dorky kid would soon see the error of his ways.

He let more people in, the same routine every time. ID, please. Kid hands him either a real ID or a clearly fake one. The stench of cheap aftershave strong in the air. Girls pasted in fake tan and wearing far too little, especially for a winter's night.

And it was worse now than ever. All thanks to the coronavirus and the gut-punch it gave to society.

Now everyone was out. Ready to get pissed up. And ready to make Max's night hard work.

At least he could get his hands on with them if they kicked off. He didn't stand for any messing, that was for sure. But it was always the Love Island, hairless chest, tight jeans, and no socks muscle-lads who wanted to take him on because they could see he was pretty well built for his age.

Two lads in tight white polo neck T-shirts stepped forward. They reeked of aftershave. Chewing gum. And they just had this look of arrogance about them, right from the off.

One of them stared at the legs of a girl standing just ahead. Muttered something to his mate.

His mate laughed. "Don't worry, Dan. I'll have those legs apart in no time."

Max gritted his teeth. He didn't like the attitude of these guys. Didn't like their confidence or their arrogance or the way they spoke about women.

And that's when he clocked these were the two guys who were giving the dorky lad a hard time a few minutes ago.

"ID, please," Max said.

The lad on the left, the taller one, with his smirk, reached into his wallet. Lifted it, held it out in front of Max. "Like I need it anyway," he said.

He lowered his driving license before Max had a chance to properly look at it.

"Come on," the guy said. Harry, according to his ID. "You can see I'm over eighteen. Let us in. Don't be a dick about it."

Max grunted. He was used to getting abuse from customers. Learned to shrug most of it off.

But there was something about this guy that just irritated him.

"And yours?" Max asked.

The other guy, Dan, reached into his back pocket with a sigh. Pulled out his driver's licence. Held it out in front of Max.

Max squinted at it. "The photo here. It's not valid."

Dan frowned. "What?"

"I said your photo. It's all smudged. Not clearly you. Unless you have any other ID, you're not coming in."

Dan laughed. Looked at Harry, who shook his head. "You serious?"

"Yeah," Max said. And he wasn't lying. Serious was one thing he was really good at being. "Can't see your ID properly; you can't come in."

"I can't believe this," Dan said. "I can't actually believe this."

"Well, you'd better believe it," Max said. "I don't make the rules. And if it is you, well. Let's just say you've not aged too well since this photo was taken."

Harry peered at Max. This look of total disdain on his face.

"You're still welcome in, of course. Your ID's fine," Max said. "Just don't kick off. I'll be keeping an eye on you."

Harry turned his nose up. "Nah. Nah, we're alright, aren't we, Dan? We'll let this power tripper here have his fun. We'll go find somewhere else. Happy new year, retard."

Harry spat on the ground, right before Max.

Max stepped forward. Clenched his fists. A few people clapped, and a few others looked on, shocked.

"Go on," Harry said. "I dare you. I dare you."

Max took a few deep breaths.

Then he stepped back.

"Miserable bastard," Harry said as he dragged his friend away. "Nobody else to spend New Year's with, so he takes it out on the lot of us."

Max gritted his jaw.

He wanted to tear that bastard's head off for that.

Because he didn't use to be miserable.

He didn't always use to be this way.

So hateful of other people.

And so angry.

He thought about Kathryn.

He thought about David.

He thought about the times they'd visit the lights together.

The Christmases they'd enjoy together.

He thought about it all, and he felt sadness deep inside.

A loneliness.

But more than anything, hatred towards other people.

Towards everyone.

He watched the two lads walk away towards a queue for another nightclub.

And he let more and more people inside this club, one by one.

He didn't pay any real attention to the talk about weird solar activity.

He didn't think much of the weird green aurora in the sky above.

He didn't think anything of it, as the lights flickered, time and time again.

CHAPTER FIVE

New Year's Eve
23:00
One Hour Before the Event...

* * *

Aoife stood at the bar, sipped her beer, and wished tonight was over already.

The music was far too loud, for one. Maybe she was just getting old. But that blaring bass, so loud it thumped right through her chest, making her feel like she was having bloody palpitations. Yeah. It wasn't her scene, that was for sure.

She didn't mean to sound such a prude. She used to be a party animal once upon a time. But that was a long time ago. The girls she lived with, all in their early twenties, seemed to forget she was closer to forty than she was their age.

Shit. That was a sobering thought.

And there was only one way to deal with a sobering thought.

She sipped more of the cocktail, taking a bigger gulp this time. Looked over at Kayleigh and the girls, all sitting in a booth lapping up the attention of a few thirsty guys. Kayleigh clearly didn't care about the band playing outside at the lights switch-on anymore, not now she was getting all this fuss. The place stunk. There was an air of sweat hanging around the place. Full of chavvy guys and slutty girls. Again, didn't mean to sound grumpy. It just wasn't her scene. And it never really ever was, in all honesty.

She'd grown up on a farm, right out in the countryside. Her dad, God rest his soul, always used to take her on camping weekends away. He'd teach her all kinds of little tips and tricks—survival, he called it. Ways to navigate the wilderness. Ways to hunt. Ways to survive.

And she'd always felt more attached to that way of life than the city life. Ever since her dad died when she was fourteen and she was forced to live with her auntie Carol, it was like something was missing from her life. She'd always idealised the city lifestyle when she was a kid. Now, after years working in the city as a solicitor and living in a flat share she could barely pay the bills for, desperately trying to get back to university for the last year, she longed for a return to a simpler life. Those weekends away with Dad. The early starts. Watching the sunrise as he stood by her side. Listening to the birdsong. And hearing stories about Mum. A mother Aoife never knew, not really. She was too young to remember when cancer took her life.

How it broke Dad. How it made him distant and cold.

But how he and Aoife always had this connection. This bond.

How she was always his girl.

As for her brother... well.

The less she thought about her older brother, the better.

"Can I get you a drink?"

Aoife looked around. She'd been in a trance for God knows how long. It was eleven now, so they were all going to pile onto the streets to watch the band, then the big lights switch-on after the countdown to New Year, soon.

But when she looked around and saw the guy standing next to her, she felt a shiver creep down her spine.

He was tall. Quite bulky. Covered in tattoos. And he was wearing this white polo neck T-shirt that looked slightly too tight for him.

"Sorry," he said. "Should probably introduce myself. The name's Harry."

He held out a hand. And knowing what men could be like, as much as she didn't want to take it, Aoife grabbed it. Shook it, just a little.

She went to pull her hand away when he pulled her towards him, just slightly, but with enough force to make her uncomfortable.

"You look gorgeous, love."

Aoife gritted her teeth. He was younger than her. Probably in his late twenties.

"Thanks," she said, pulling her hand away.

"About that drink."

"What about it?" Aoife asked.

"What do you want?"

She smiled at him. "I'm okay. Really. But have a good night."

Harry tutted. Shook his head. "See, you don't look like a girl who *doesn't* want a drink. You look like a girl who wants to party. Who wants to dance. And then maybe, just maybe, a girl who wants to get out of here."

Aoife looked around at Harry. Narrowed her eyes. "How many other 'girls' have you peddled that vaguely rapey, consent-muddying line to, Harry?"

He frowned. Looked a little stunned, like he wasn't used to any kind of kickback like that. "What're you trying to say?"

"I'm trying to say I'm not interested, sunshine. Now bugger off. Go bother somebody else. I don't like your bullshit. And I'm here to have a drink and then get the hell out of here as soon as I possibly can, but not with you. So go on. Shoo. You look like you've had one too many."

He stood there. And for a few seconds, as his face turned redder and redder in the nightclub lights, Aoife wondered if he might just explode.

But then he puffed out his lips. Shook his head.

And then he barged past her.

"Your friends said you were a frigid nun who needs to get the hell over your ex."

She heard those words, and they froze her, just for a moment.

"What—what did you just say?"

He looked around at her as he walked. Looked at her with utter disdain.

Then he disappeared out into the crowd, into the midst of the dancing bodies.

She stood there for a while, not totally sure how long. And she just kept on hearing what that guy, Harry, said to her.

Your friends said you were a frigid nun who needs to get the hell over your ex.

Why would they say that?

She looked around to where her flatmates were, with their friends. Saw them all peering over. Saw Kayleigh roll her eyes, mutter something to a blonde bimbo by her side. The way she nodded, rolled her eyes back.

And she knew what they were saying.

She could hear their conversation without having to *actually* hear it.

She knew they were picking holes in her relationship with Jason.

With her marriage.

But if they knew the truth, the whole truth about everything that'd happened and everything she'd been through, maybe they'd be a bit more sensitive.

"I'm out of here," she muttered. She wasn't sure whether it was drink. She didn't know what it was.

But she was done trying to please these people.

She gulped down the rest of her cocktail, planted it on the bar, then walked past the mass of people towards the exit.

* * *

FOR JUST ONE SPLIT SECOND, every light in the nightclub went out for a little longer than they should, then flickered back on again.

Nobody noticed.

CHAPTER SIX

New Year's Eve
23:55
Five Minutes Before the Event...

* * *

"Come on. Come on, now. No messing around. Out onto the streets. Take it easy. No need for any pushing."

Max herded the people out of the nightclub and onto the streets for the big lights switch-on. At least, the ones who were still left in the club, anyway. There weren't many now. The vast majority of people had flooded out an hour ago to watch the band, but naturally, there were a few stubborn gits in here.

And unfortunately for Max, those who remained were amongst the drunkest of the lot.

He'd listened to the band, and they were shit. Spent ages standing out here, teeth chattering, freezing his balls off. One of the other security guards, Malcolm, tried chatting to him a bit back. But he wasn't really listening. Not really in the mood for chit-chat.

Hell. Was he ever?

Yeah, actually. Back when Kathryn was alive. Used to be quite talkative back then. Quite the life of the party.

But shit. That was a long, long time ago.

He thought about what that dickhead he'd not allowed in the club said earlier. About him spending New Year on his own. And there was something about those remarks that bothered him. That really got under his skin.

And as he ushered more and more people out of this nightclub and towards the big switch on, he wondered if maybe it's because the guy had a point.

Maybe he was just taking his frustrations out on other people because of the things that happened to him.

He thought about Kathryn. Of David.

He thought about when he was working night shifts as a police officer.

Getting home and seeing all the blood.

Hearing the scream.

And seeing the look in those piercing blue eyes of the man standing over...

No.

He shook his head. Shivered. He didn't want to think about that. Not right now.

He looked around. Saw the dorky guy with the glasses stumbling out. The kid he'd let in earlier, clearly underage. The guy looked worse for wear. And as much as this kid irritated Max, he found himself wanting to check on him. Make sure he was okay. Especially seeing as he didn't seem to be with any friends.

"You okay, kid?"

The kid looked around at Max. Glared at him with drifting eyes. "Me? I..."

And then he vomited on the ground, right before Max's feet.

Max sighed. He wanted to tell the kid to keep moving. But he felt a bit responsible. He was clearly underage. He'd let him in the club, and he'd got drunk.

But still. He was old enough to look after himself.

"Come on," Max said. "Let's get you in a taxi."

He hailed a cab, clearly grateful for early business before the mad rush later. Helped the lad onto the back seat, much to the disapproval of the driver, who seemed panicked about just how sick this kid was.

"You'll thank me for it later. Just don't vomit on the driver's seats or you're on your own."

He patted the side of the cab and watched it disappear down the road, then turned his attention to the stage.

He could see it, right there in the distance. Someone on stage with a microphone telling shitty jokes. And as he stood there and looked at all these people, it amazed him to see humanity back together again after the COVID pandemic. People coming together. Society functioning as it used to, once more.

And as much as he hated people... he got it. Really. They'd waited a long time for a good night out like this. A night out without rules or restrictions.

He wondered where he'd be right now if Kathryn were still here. If David were still here.

He swallowed a lump in his throat.

He had to stop with this sentimental shit.

Had to focus on his job.

The club behind him looked empty, but the lights were still flashing. The whole street was lit up, but nothing compared to what it would look like soon when the New Year's lights came on, and the fireworks erupted. They'd made an extra big deal this year. Christmas Lights *and* New Year's lights. Apparently, the council was worried about the whole thing overpowering the electricity boards and causing a power surge across town.

But hell. It was New Year. They'd get it fixed. Get it back online.

Anything to lift the spirits of Preston's residents after a tough few years.

Obviously a load of crap as far as Max was concerned. Get your countdown done, do your fireworks if you absolutely have to, then get a bit drunker before collapsing in bed and cracking on with another miserable year ahead.

That was the reality.

He looked at the sea of people standing in front of the stage. Looked at the man standing on there, some budget celebrity from Burnley, apparently. A reality TV "star." Clearly not much of a star because Max hadn't heard of him. Wondered if anyone had. Or if anyone really even cared.

"Great, ain't it?"

Max looked around. Saw Malcolm, his colleague, beside him. "What is?"

Malcolm stood there, smile on his face. Older chap. Grey. Annoying as hell, and never knew when to shut up. "Seeing 'em. Seeing 'em all enjoying themselves. It's as if nothing ever happened with the COVID stuff. It's as if things are normal again. And things are always gonna be normal, from this point on. Because people. People coming together. That's what matters most, huh? That's what matters more than anything."

Max grunted. And then he turned his attention to the countdown, which was well underway now.

"Ten! Nine! Eight!"

He saw himself in Paris with Kathryn at New Year. One of the lucky ones to make it to the top of the Eiffel Tower that night, all via a raffle at work.

"Seven! Six! Five!"

He saw her laughing as he got on one knee.

"Four! Three!"

How gorgeous she looked when he proposed to her.

"Two!"

I do, Max. I do.

"One!"
David in her arms, the pride, the joy, the—
"Happy New Year!"
A flash.
A sudden bolt of light, brighter than Max expected.
And then darkness.

CHAPTER SEVEN

New Year's Eve
23:56
Four Minutes Before the Event...

* * *

Aoife sat on the bus and wanted more than anything to just get back to the house.

Coming out with the girls was a mistake. A terrible mistake. They were bitching about her behind her back. Trying to set her up with that polo-necked creep at the bar, by the looks of things. She was done trying to please them at this point. At the end of the day, they were just younger than her. They didn't have the same life experience as her.

And sure. Maybe she *did* look down on them a little bit, something she'd been in denial about until this point. But perhaps it wasn't without good reason. At the end of the day, they were immature. And they'd proven their immaturity to her tonight.

She cursed herself for ever coming out tonight. She could've stayed at home and got another application or two done. What was the point getting all melodramatic about New Year, anyway? People treated it like it was some special event, some marker that everything was going to change. New Year, New Me. Resolutions. New habits, all to be dropped in a matter of weeks.

Well, she could play that game, but she was going to play it properly.

She was getting out of that flat share.

She was going to university.

She wasn't going to keep on failing the way she'd failed the last few years.

She thought about her job as a solicitor. How it'd all fallen apart. The late nights. The stress. And the event that ultimately led to her walking away.

But really, she had been looking for an opportunity to get out for years. It was a well-paid job, of course. Very secure. Exactly the kind of job she should be proud of.

And she was proud of it. Proud that she'd managed to work her way so far to the top as a young woman.

But she didn't feel like it was the path she wanted to go down, not really. There was a better path out there for her. There had to be.

And if there wasn't, well, that was just a miserable thought she was going to have to live with.

She thought about Jason again. How good things had seemed.

But how much things fell apart.

The arguments.

The hysterics.

And eventually, the breakup, and all that prompted it.

She shook her head. Took a deep breath.

That was the past now. She didn't have to worry about it anymore.

She looked around the bus. It was empty. Just her and the driver. It smelled a bit of urine on here. The windows were all dusty and steamed up. She could see people outside, all smiling, all having a laugh, and it was like she was looking at an exhibit of a life she used to live. Of a happiness she used to feel.

She turned away. She didn't want to see that. She didn't need any reminders.

She glanced at her watch. A couple of minutes to midnight. She knew the fireworks would all start soon. She could still hear the music from town, the vague notes of someone shouting down a megaphone. She could hear it all, and she wanted to get away from it. To stuff her headphones on and drown it all out.

She was independent. She could make it on her own.

She didn't know why she was suddenly feeling so down about things. Best to just lift her chin up and power on like Dad always used to tell her when she suffered a setback.

She saw the bus indicating into the bus stop and noticed someone at the door.

She recognised him. Wasn't sure where from, not at first.

But when he got on, her heart sank.

It was the guy from the nightclub. Harry.

"Single to Grimsargh, please."

He turned around, wandered onto the bus, looking somewhat pissed off, and then his eyes met Aoife's.

Don't recognise me, don't recognise me, don't...

"Oh, hey. Fancy seeing you here."

Suddenly, he didn't look pissed off. His eyes lit up. Like he had something new to focus on.

Aoife looked away and didn't say a word. Best to just ignore him.

He sat down, right in front of her. Leaned against the back of his seat, staring at her. He stunk of booze, and he had beer right down his shirt.

"You know, I've had a shitty night," he said.

"I feel bad for you."

"I've been barred from entering one place because the bouncer was a prick to my mate. I've been kicked out of another place for scrapping. And all the birds here... they're all frigid as hell. But nothing's pissed me off more than the way you spoke to me. Nothing."

Aoife turned and looked at him. He was bigger than her and might think he was stronger than her. But she knew how to defend herself if need be.

"I'm sorry my words offended your almighty ego. It must really hurt, being rejected. You seem like you're not used to hearing a few home truths."

His face turned sour. His nose twitched. "You're a bitch. You know that?"

"Hear you loud and clear."

"You're—you're a nasty, ugly bitch. I only paid any attention to you because I felt sorry for you. Because of this boo-hoo nasty breakup of yours your friends told me about. Thought you looked alright behind the beer goggles. But you're not alright. You're ugly. And I can't believe I ever gave you the time of day."

"Then leave me alone," Aoife said, on the verge of exploding with anger. "Leave me alone and go sit somewhere else. I'm sure there'll be plenty of other girls out there for you to harass."

He spat on Aoife. Right on her face, out of nowhere. A big blob of phlegm, drooling down her face.

She wiped it away, rage seething through her. "You—you disgusting piece of shit."

Harry smiled at her. "That's it. The real nasty girl coming out. That's what I like to see—"

She swiped him with her nails. She knew she shouldn't, but she did, and she did it hard.

So hard he was bleeding.

From his face.

And his right eye was all bloodshot.

"You bitch!" he shouted.

And in the moment of anger, of adrenaline, the pair of them didn't even notice the fireworks.

He looked at her with total rage.

"You'll pay for this. You'll..."

She wasn't sure if he said anything else.

Because all the lights on the bus went off.

The driver shouted something.

And the next thing Aoife knew, she heard a massive crash, and she hurtled out of her seat and into the darkness.

CHAPTER EIGHT

New Year's Eve
23:57
Three Minutes Before the Event...

* * *

Cassandra Peterson didn't think much about the palpitations in her chest as she ran down her street in the darkness.

She was always getting palpitations these days. A by-product of the anti-anxiety medication she was on, apparently. Ironic, really. Palpitations were a very real source of anxiety for sufferers. So a pill that *gives* people palpitations? What a cruel irony.

But she was getting better. She was beginning to ride them out, to heal.

And one of the key parts of her recovery was exercise.

She ran down the street. It was a quiet suburban neighbourhood, the kind where you never had to worry about any sort of trouble, any kind of crime. She preferred running at night because she felt like fewer eyes were on her. Sure, she knew what her doctor would say. *Push yourself! Challenge yourself! Throw yourself into uncomfortable situations!*

But Cassandra wasn't ready for that step. And regardless, she did actually enjoy running late at night, as much as Mum and Dad always told her she was crazy for doing so.

She felt her chest tightening a little, then loosened her focus on it and let it go. There were so many ways she'd learned to help control the anxiety. To help relax herself. She wasn't sure what triggered it. She'd never been an anxious person. She was in her late twenties now and never had any real concerns. No real serious relationships. A steady job as an accountant.

But she guessed there *had* been a few changes. The pandemic, COVID-19. The isolation. The loneliness.

Moving back in with her parents was definitely a good idea. She always told herself she'd get back to normal and go see her friends again when it all eased. But that didn't happen. Suddenly, she was afraid to do things she used to take so for granted.

And so began her long road to recovery.

She thought about how much better she was starting to feel lately, as one foot landed in front of the other. Thought about getting back to working from the office rather than from home. She thought about seeing her friends again. Going out. Drinking. Having a laugh.

And then she felt a flicker of sadness inside.

It was New Year's Eve. A night she always used to be out, whether at a house party or in a crammed pub. She'd had a few invites to places, but she'd passed on them all.

Because she just didn't feel up to it yet. She didn't quite feel *ready*.

And moments like that, moments of defeat, they made her feel a little sad. A little defeated. Made her feel like she wasn't making progress or was going backwards.

But then she took a few deep breaths.

Calmed herself.

She was okay.

She was on the road to recovery.

It wasn't going to be instant. It wasn't going to be overnight. But she was going to do this.

She went to turn a corner when she felt another twinge in her chest.

Her mouth went dry, just for a moment. Because this twinge, it felt stronger than a palpitation. Heavier.

She thought about the operation she'd had as a young kid. A rare heart defect requiring a pacemaker. But it's the way she'd always been. She'd never had to think about it, not really. It'd never caused her any problems.

And sure. She knew she was different. She knew she wasn't like the other kids. Especially with the scar above her collarbone where they'd inserted it. Used to get funny looks in P.E. at school. A few whispers behind her back and glimpses of disgust.

But she didn't mope about it. Didn't dwell on it.

She just got on with her life.

But this pain, right now. For some reason, she wondered. Even though she'd been to the hospital, and they'd insisted her heart rhythm was normal and everything was in order... what if something was different now?

What if something was *wrong?*

She swallowed a lump in her throat.

You're just being paranoid. You're absolutely fine. It's nothing to worry about.

She went to start up running again when something happened.

It was so instant.

First, the fireworks, making her jump out of her skin.

The cacophony of light above.

But also something else.

Something stranger.

Something weirder.

The lights all around her.

The streetlamp.

The lights inside houses.

Just as the roar of "Happy New Year!" went up, those lights dropped.

She stood there a few seconds. Sweating. Heart racing. A weird ghostliness to the air. A sense of unease. Like something just wasn't right.

That's when she felt the pain in her chest.

Like an explosion.

That's when she felt the palpitation; the palpitation that felt stronger than any she'd ever had.

And that's when she collapsed to the road, and everything went black.

CHAPTER NINE

New Year's Eve
23:58
Two Minutes Before the Event...

* * *

Christian Hart sat by the side of his father's hospital bed and prayed for a better year ahead.

It was late at night, but it could be any time of day at all. He'd spent so long in here that the boundary between day and night didn't really mean anything at all. The critical care ward was in the basement area of Preston Hospital, so there was no daylight in here. Just a screen over at the far side of the room, where a bright artificial white light pumped in constantly, not fooling anyone with its false illusion of the day.

Christian sat by his father's bedside. He wanted to hold his hand, but he couldn't because he was advised not to. He listened to the bleeping of the life support machines. Watched his father's chest rise and fall as the life support machine kept him alive in his state of unconsciousness. And he wanted to speak to him. He wanted to say so many things to him. Wanted to talk about the times when they spent playing football when he was growing up. Or the late nights playing Tekken on PlayStation when Mum was sleeping. He wanted to talk about so many things.

But he couldn't. Because it was pointless. He heard the talks of people chatting to relatives in comas. The rumours that it was "good for them" based on some pitiful human ideation that everything was within our control even when it really wasn't.

He should know. He'd studied medicine. He knew an induced coma was a state of total nothingness. When people spoke about dreams they had when they were under, they were mostly referring to the final stages when they were coming round and being woken up.

The other state?

Total blackness.

And yet, there was something peaceful about that state. Something reassuring to Christian, knowing his dear father wasn't suffering. That he wasn't going through nightmares. That all of this would pass like a finger click, and before he knew it, he'd be back up and on his feet again.

"You're going to get better, Dad," Christian whispered. Realising right away he was breaking his own policy of not talking. "You're going to make it."

No response from his father.

Just the rise and fall of his chest, again, again, again.

Christian thought about his dad's final few years. How sad they'd been. The fallout with Anya, Christian's sister, over something so petty Christian could barely remember it. But the pair of them were stubborn to the point of never resolving their differences.

Christian remembered ringing Anya when Dad caught pneumonia, which eventually descended into sepsis in hospital after a routine operation. Telling her about him, how he was going into intensive care. Asking her to come down and see him before he went under because God knows whether he'd wake up again.

She acted upset. Said all the right things.

But she never turned up.

And Christian hadn't been able to get hold of her since.

So Dad went under with just Christian by his side.

He looked up at Christian before he'd gone under with a smile on his face. And Christian looked back at him. "What you smiling about?"

Dad smiled back at him. Shook his head.

"Go on. You'd better tell me now. You're not going to be so chatty for the next couple of days."

He looked around at Christian, tightened his grip on his hand, and he smiled.

"I'm proud of you, son. And no matter what happens here... I know I won't be alone. I know you'll be here. Always."

Christian felt a tear creep down his cheek as he sat there beside his dad. He knew he didn't have long in critical care. But it was better than during the coronavirus pandemic, where you weren't even allowed to visit a relative.

He looked along the rest of the bodies in their states of suspended animation. Saw a nurse washing the forehead of a woman a few beds down with such tenderness, such care.

He saw it all, and then he heard the fireworks from above.

His first thought: oh, shit. It's New Year. Would you believe it?

His second?

The lights went out.

Just for a moment, everything seemed to stop.

Everything went black.

The bleeping stopped.

The machines stopped.

And outside, the fireworks went off.

And then, a split second later, the machines were back on

again. Although there was a louder noise this time. The generator kicking in, clearly.

One of the nurses looked over at Christian. Smiled. "It'll be okay, love. Power outage. We've got good generators here. All be back online in no time."

Christian nodded. Looked back at his dad, who was breathing away with assistance again.

He had no idea of what was ahead.

And he had no idea that the generators only had 96 hours of fuel left before the power ran out completely.

CHAPTER TEN

New Year's Eve
23:59
One Minute Before the Event...

* * *

Michaela Harrison stood in the elevator of her apartment and wanted nothing more than to get back home.

It'd been a shocking night. First off, she'd seen Dave, her boyfriend, getting off with another girl. And as much as he insisted it was just a laugh, she wasn't buying any of it. She knew what she'd seen. He was a dickhead. He did it all the time, even though he insisted he loved her, and it was only her he cared about.

She stood there, tears stinging her eyes. A slight taste of nausea and vomit in her mouth. Hammering the button to take her back to the fourth floor and wondering if she should take the stairs instead.

"Stupid thing," she said, her head spinning a little. She hated the spins. Always got them when she'd had too much to drink. "Always jamming when I need you to work. Why can't you just *work?*"

She hit the "up" button a few more times before finally sighing and giving up.

She went to step out of the elevator when the doors suddenly slammed shut on her.

She stepped back, sighed. Rubbed her fingers against her temples. She felt so sick. So rough. She just wanted to get back. Back to bed. She knew she'd regret missing the fireworks in the morning. Knew she'd feel awful for missing seeing in the new year with her friends.

But they always said she had a penchant for being dramatic when she was drunk. And as much as she denied it, she figured they had a point.

"I just want my bed," she muttered. "I just want to get back and get to my bed and..."

The elevator stopped.

The lights flickered, just for a moment.

A moment's horror. Total terror.

Then the door opened.

She was about to roll her eyes and curse under her breath when she saw a guy wander in.

"Sorry," he said, smile on his face. "Got off at the wrong floor."

He was handsome. That's the first thought that struck Michaela. Handsome. Not "fit" or "buff" but handsome. Tall. Black. Short hair, looked well-groomed. Dark brown eyes and this beaming smile that made her shake at the knees a little bit. Holding on to this rucksack, which looked heavy.

So despite her annoyance, her irritation, and her drunkenness, she smiled back. "Sure. No problem. Which floor you heading to?"

"Fourth floor," he said.

"Oh. Fourth floor. Same as me!"

He nodded, smiled. Smelled... expensive. Like good quality aftershave. Not the cheap shit most lads wore. Dave being one of them, dare she say it.

And she knew it was wrong to be feeling this way about a total stranger. She knew it was unfaithful to even flirt with somebody. And she knew how glaring her own double standards were here.

But she was drunk, and she was pissed with Dave, so hell, yeah, was she going to flirt a bit.

"So," she said, fluttering her eyelashes. "What're you doing here on a night like tonight?"

He turned to her. Frowned. "A night like tonight?"

"New Year's Eve."

"Oh! Oh, yeah. Sorry. I, erm. Well. I guess I just moved here recently. So not got many, y'know. Friends."

"Oh," Michaela said. "I'm sorry. That sounds kind of... sad."

"Well, that's me. Sad Oliver."

"Oliver. Nice to meet you. I'm Michaela."

He held out a hand, which Michaela took. Tough, but soft enough to feel respectful, too. "You can call me Oli."

That beaming smile that melted her from within.

"So, I'll ask another question," she said.

"Fire away."

"You don't know anyone. So what're you doing here?"

Oli rolled his eyes, smiled some more with that drop-dead gorgeous smile. "Oh. I'm doing a delivery."

"Delivery?"

"Yeah," he said, holding up his bag. "UberEats."

"Oh," Michaela said. "I use UberEats all the time. Shame we've never met before."

"Well, we can meet again some time. If you fancy?"

She looked into his eyes, and she smiled. She liked his confidence. But what she liked most was that even though they were in what could be seen as a pretty threatening setting for a woman on her own, she didn't feel intimidated by this guy. Not remotely.

"Sorry," he said. "I shouldn't have suggested that. It's... it's not really appropriate, is it?"

"No," she said. "But not for the reasons you might think."

"Oh?"

"I've..."

She was going to tell him she had a boyfriend.

Then she saw Dave flash in her mind, tongue down the throat of whatever slag slapped up in fake tan came before him.

"Actually," she said. "Forget I ever said anything. It'd be great to see you again sometime."

She pulled out her phone, shaking with the adrenaline of what she knew was a sin.

Held it in front of her.

"My number," she said, fully aware she sounded a bit eager. "It's..."

And then something weird happened.

Her phone died right then.

"Weird," she said. "My phone. It just froze."

"That's odd," Oli said. "Mine's the... mine's the same."

She looked up at Oli. Saw the concern in his eyes. Felt the weirdness as they stood there in this lift.

"Hope it's nothing to do with that weird solar storm," Oli said.

"What weird solar storm?"

"You know. The one they're on about on the news. Wouldn't have thought anything of it. But then I wouldn't have thought anything of a global pandemic threat and look what happened there."

The thought scared her, just for a moment. A solar storm. She didn't know what the hell one of those was, but it didn't sound good.

"Well, it's a good job I've got you here to look after me, isn't it?"

He smiled back at her.

She knew this was wrong.

Very wrong.

But she wanted to kiss him.

She wanted—

The lights of the lift went out.

Everything stopped.

"What..."

And then she felt the lift give way and hurtle down.

Fast.

So fast she could barely even hear herself scream.

And as she plummeted below, all she could think of was that this was punishment for contemplating cheating on Dave.

And then the smell of the fries in Oli's delivery bag.

And then his shouts and cries and her own screams and—

A bang.

Then, nothing.

CHAPTER ELEVEN

New Year's Day
00:00

* * *

It all happened so fast.
One second, the countdown ended.
The crowd erupted, cheering.
The guy switching the lights on hit that button, and for a moment, just for a solitary moment, there was light. Bright light, illuminating the entire square of Preston City Centre that people were crammed into, as Max stood there, watching.
One second, light.
Then a bang.
All the lights went out.
A few screams went out. Laughter. But more than anything, fireworks. Fireworks erupting into the night sky, lighting everything up. And everyone just stared up there as a few people groaned. The lights had gone out. The music had gone out.

And the more Max looked around, the more he realised something else.

The lights. All the street lamps. All the lights outside the shops. Or in the houses and the flats. All of them had gone out, leaving total darkness.

He stood there and looked at the crowd of people before him. The bulk of them pointing their phone cameras up at the sky, something that really annoyed him. Why not get right in the moment instead of recording it for bloody Snapchat or whatever it was called? Why live life through a screen?

After all, who the fuck even cared about the fireworks if they weren't there? One of humanity's greatest delusions, that. The misguided belief that other people really gave a shit about their crap.

Why bother recording a gig of a band somebody else doesn't even give a shit about—and then go on to bore them to death by making them watch it?

People were so full of themselves.

But right now, Max noticed something different. Something unusual. Something odd, amidst the erupting blast of the fireworks, the flashes in the sky.

The phone screens. They were black. All of them were dead.

A few people lowered them, looked at them. Hit the power button. Tried to switch them on again. But nobody was having any luck, by the looks of things.

And Max had to admit there was something weird about it. His first thought when the lights had burst and the power had tripped was that the electrical grid was down. There'd been a lot of talk about it from the council, especially having already got the Christmas lights plugged in. Fears of an overload. But fears they were going to ignore anyway because they wanted people to really enjoy New Year and put on the biggest show after all the COVID shit last year.

Really, Max knew that just meant they were struggling for cash and wanted an excuse to charge an extortionate amount for residents to watch a shit, Z-list band, probably a mate of the council leader's wife, and rake a bit more money into the pockets of the higher-ups around here after a challenging year.

But now, seeing all these phones out and all the confusion that came with it... he had a weird feeling about everything.

Something didn't seem right.

He heard the chatter. Heard the shouting. Heard the nervous laughter. And most of all, he heard the tension. Because it seemed like literally everybody's phone was out here.

And humanity wasn't supposed to be disconnected. Not anymore. Not when you had notifications for everything. Not when you had the government basically running you via your smartphone. Not when you had this window to the world in the palm of your hands at all times.

Max remembered his dad telling him tales of how everyone was going to be "microchipped" one day. How it would be billed as a way of making things easier—infinite access to information, payment methods linked to the person and not a cheap little card, that sort of thing.

But really, it was a way of spying. A way of keeping tabs. A way of making people reliant.

Max was always sceptical. He figured humanity would never sign up to an experiment like that in their droves.

Turns out they didn't need microchips planting under their skin, after all.

Mobile phones had been the Trojan horse for that whole exercise.

He reached into his pocket for his old Nokia, a phone he barely used. Only ever used it for calls, mostly work-related. Couldn't be bothered with any texting or social media or anything like that. That wasn't his world.

But when he lifted his phone out of his pocket and saw it was dead, too, he started to get an even weirder feeling about all this.

"It's the solar flare," someone muttered. "You saw the weird lights earlier, right? Solar flare's taken all our electricity out. We're fucked. We're utterly fucked."

He sounded panicked. But the sorts of glances he was getting were those a madman talking about the end being nigh would get in the streets. Nobody was taking him seriously, even though all the proof Max could see suggested...

No.

There couldn't be a coronal mass ejection. Or an electromagnetic pulse event.

It might be a possibility. But it wasn't something that was *actually* going to happen.

It was something reserved for the realms of science-fiction.

Right?

What, just like the global pandemic?

He heard a few shouts, then. A few shouts off in the distance. Shouts of panic.

A girl, tears streaming down her face, her eyes wide. Crouched by the side of a guy who looked like he'd passed out.

"He just collapsed!" she said. "When—when the lights went out. He just collapsed and—and I don't think his heart's beating. Someone help. I can't ring an ambulance. Please!"

Max saw all the confusion turning to panic in an instant, as fireworks continued to explode above.

He looked around, away from the main square. Over towards the city centre.

Saw the taxis sitting there, unable to budge.

Drivers shouting to one another as they tried to get their phones working.

He saw the darkness, and he wondered...

Could it be?

Could it...

That's when he heard it.

So sudden.

A screeching sound.

Something hurtling closer.

He looked around and saw it in slow motion.

Over by the train tracks, which stretched above this section of the city.

A train flying into the station.

All its lights off.

Not slowing down.

Not…

"It's gonna crash!" someone shouted.

The next thing, Max saw a huge eruption of light.

Felt a wave of heat.

And then he heard the bang.

CHAPTER TWELVE

New Year's Day
00:00

* * *

First, total darkness.
Then, agony.
Aoife opened her mouth and gasped. It hurt to breathe. It hurt to *anything*. Her body ached everywhere. Even the slightest movement made her wince with pain. Her head banged with pain, like a thousand needles were shaking around in there every time she moved it. She could hear ringing, like an alarm siren, but she wasn't sure if it was an alarm or if she'd hit her head. Hard.

Where was she? That's the first thought she had. She had memories. Blurry memories. Memories of working on her university applications. Then memories of being out. In a nightclub. Partying. Wanting to get the hell out of there. Drinking. Being approached at the bar by a creep called Harry.

Then heading back. Jumping on the bus.

And then Harry getting on the bus and...

First, she remembered the way he'd spoken to her. She remembered his anger at her rejection. And she remembered what he'd said to her to piss her off. To make her swipe her nails into his face.

"You're a nasty, ugly bitch. I only paid any attention to you because I felt sorry for you. Because of your break-up..."

But after that... there was a blank. Fireworks, darkness, and a blank.

She couldn't remember what happened after that, and it scared her.

She opened her eyes again.

Her eyes were stinging like mad. It felt like she was staring into a bright light, but she soon realised she was surrounded by total darkness. She could hear something. Something like rustling. She could feel a warmth, too. A warmth that was getting warmer. And every single breath made her want to choke and vomit.

She looked around, tried to make sense of her surroundings. She was lying on the floor, on her side. Only there was ice beneath her. Loads of cracked ice all around her, only it didn't feel cold. It felt...

She blinked a few times and soon realised she wasn't lying on a bed of ice.

It was glass. Broken glass.

She looked around, and suddenly, her surroundings clicked; suddenly, she made sense of them.

She was still in the bus. Only the bus had flipped onto its side. She was lying on the smashed remains of the windows. Her hands were all cut, and there was something heavy pressing down on top of her.

She turned around to try and free herself from the weight above her when she realised exactly what it was.

Or rather, *who* it was.

It was Harry. The creep who'd asked to get her a drink in the bar then followed her onto the bus. His eyes were closed. His face was covered in thin streams of blood.

Aoife let out a scream. But screaming hurt and took what little energy she had out of her. Was he dead? Shit. There'd been a crash. There'd been some sort of crash, and she was trapped here. She was trapped and she was scared and...

Don't worry. Stay calm. There's been a crash, which means there'll be ambulances here soon. They'll help you out of this. They'll free you. Don't worry.

She breathed as deeply as she could, but she was shaking all over. Adrenaline surged through her system. She had to be careful moving too quickly or suddenly. God knows how many bones she'd broken, or worse. She remembered Auntie Carol telling her a story once about when Dad stepped on a nail going down to the basement in their old holiday cottage. How he felt this nasty pain but didn't realise quite how bad it was until he saw the end of the nail poking out of it. And even then, he just thought he'd snapped a bit of it off. Not a full three-inch nail wedged right into the base of his foot.

She knew the most logical thing was to wait here. To take deep breaths and be patient. Even though she was terrified and even though she wanted to get out of here as soon as possible, she didn't want to do any more damage on top of the damage she'd already done.

She lay there. Heart racing. Shaking. Harry lying on top of her, so heavy, so suffocating.

You're going to be okay. Just take deep breaths. Just take deep breaths, stay calm, and everything is going to be okay...

She lay there for God knows how long. It felt like hours, but it could be minutes. And she didn't hear any sirens. She didn't hear any ambulances. Or any cars at all, for that matter.

She wanted to look out of the window, but she couldn't see a thing because the bus was on its side. And she couldn't turn around because of Harry's weight on top of her. Why couldn't she hear anything? Why wasn't anyone coming to help her?

"Help!" she shouted, feeling pitiful and desperate. She never liked coming across as helpless or weak. She'd always preferred to fend for herself, to go her own way. Didn't like to be too reliant on other people. Anyway, as aloof as it sounded, she usually knew best. Other opinions just held her back and dragged her down. Better to just trust her own instincts and do her own thing. It'd usually got her further in life.

But nobody responded.

She felt anger creeping in. A bus crash, right in a well-populated area, and nobody was coming to help her?

What the hell was happening out there?

She closed her eyes. Battled to keep calm.

But in the end, she couldn't help herself; couldn't resist.

"Someone, help!"

But again, her crackly, broken voice just echoed through the bus.

Echoed out into the darkness.

Into nothingness.

She felt tears in her eyes. Because despite everything, she wanted Jason here.

He'd know what to do.

He'd look after her.

He'd help her.

She imagined he was right here beside her, the weight of Harry's body pressing down on her when she saw something flickering up ahead.

She lifted her head. Frowned.

When she realised what it was, her stomach turned.

There was a fire in the bus.

And it was coming her way.

CHAPTER THIRTEEN

Max heard the bang, saw the massive flash of light, and felt the earth-shattering, ground-shaking eruption of energy crash against him.

He was blinded very suddenly by bright light. The coldness of the New Year's air suddenly became hot. It hurt to breathe. His ears rang. He swore he could hear screaming, but he wasn't too sure.

Just the ringing in his ears, as he blinked, totally disoriented, trying to make sense of his surroundings, trying to figure out where he was and what the hell just happened.

He blinked a few times, tried to get his sight back, tried to see.

That's when he saw it.

His vision returned. He could see something up above. Over by the train line, which ran over the section of the city they were in.

Something had happened.

A train. It'd collided into the station; smashed into another train.

And...

He stood there, and he froze completely.

The train above was burning away—badly. There were people in that train. People behind the windows. People banging against the glass, trying to escape. Struggling at the doors.

And as Max looked up there, all he could do was stand. All he could do was stare. There was nothing else he could do. Because those flames. They were so strong. And there were so many of them.

He wasn't sure anyone could do a thing.

He looked on the ground around him. A woman lay on the road. Her head was bleeding, a large chunk of metal by her side, which had clearly detached and flown down towards her. More chunks of debris scattered around. Blood. People lying dead in the middle of the streets. A few security guards trying to control the situation, to abate the panic, but not doing a very good job.

They looked just as lost as everyone.

Just as panicked as everyone.

"We need an ambulance down here!" an old bloke shouted. "There's—there's so many injured. And that train."

"We'd get an ambulance if we could ring 'em," one of the security guards shouted.

Max looked around and saw a few police officers running down the street, then. But he could tell from the look on their faces and the fact they were on foot that they were just as lost as everybody here. They were just as confused as everybody here. As scared as everybody here.

And it began to dawn on him, as he stood there, that maybe his fears were right.

Maybe his suspicions were right.

Maybe this was exactly what it looked like.

He heard a scream over to the left. Looked around. Saw a woman and a baby on that train. The woman was holding the baby towards the window as the flames crept through it. Both of them were covered in blood.

And seeing them there, seeing the woman's desperation... as much as Max knew, the safest and most logical thing to do right now was to get the hell away from here; there was no way he was turning away. There was no way he was turning his back on this woman. Not a cat in hell's chance.

He tightened his jaw. His fists. Took a deep breath.

And then he raced towards the platform.

He ran. Ran past people who were collapsed on the side of the street. Ran through people struggling with their phones, trying to get them working all in vain. He ran, and he knew this was mad. He knew it was a suicide mission.

But that woman.

That woman with her baby...

He got a flash.

A flash back to the night he'd got back home from work.

The night he'd found Kathryn lying there, sitting against the kitchen island, in a pool of blood.

How she'd told him to save him.

David. Save him, Max. Save him.

And then racing into David's bedroom and...

No.

He couldn't go there.

He couldn't think about that. Not now.

He ran up the stairs. People rushed past him, people covered in blood, people who had managed to escape the train.

"You don't want to go that way, buddy," an Asian guy said, cuts and bruises all over his face.

"I do," Max said. "I've got to."

He ran to the top of the platform; then, he crossed over. The closer he got to the train, the more he could feel that heat growing more and more intense, stronger and stronger. And the more he questioned whether this was what he really wanted to do.

But it wasn't a case of "want." It was a case of what he *had* to do.

And was there an element of making up for the past involved? No.

He couldn't think like that.

He just had to get to that window.

He had to get to that woman.

He had to save that kid.

He raced down the steps, passed more people who had managed to fight their way out of one of the train carriages. The heat was so hot. Searing. Like standing in the middle of a bonfire, let alone the side of one.

And the smoke, too. The smoke was getting thicker. Getting on his chest. A few people lay dead at the side of the platform.

And still there were no signs of medical crew.

Still, there were no signs of help.

He ran to the end of the platform. Then he clambered down onto the tracks, crossed over to the other side.

And then he ran down the side of the train, desperately searching for that woman and her child, desperately trying to find her again.

He looked through the train's smoke-filled windows and saw all kinds of horrors. People lying dead already. People barely even recognisable as people anymore, especially with how twisted and contorted their bodies were.

So much blood.

So much death.

He kept running down the side of the train. He swore that woman had to be close. He kept on going and going, as much as he knew he needed to get away from here soon, as much as he knew he needed to get away—fast.

He kept going when he saw her.

She was standing at the window. Tears and blood streaming down her face.

Baby in her arms, crying.

"Please," she begged as smoke filled the cabin. "Take him. Save him. Please."

Max heard those words, and his whole world stood still.

Save him. Please.

Opening the bedroom door.

Finding...

No.

He pulled back his fist. Slammed it into the glass.

Then he punched again. Again. Again.

Kept on punching repeatedly.

He had to break through.

He had to help this kid.

And he had to help the kid's mother, too, if he could.

He kept on going as the glass got hotter.

As the tracks started to creak and grow unsteady.

He kept on going as the flames grew taller.

As his escape route disappeared before his eyes.

He kept on punching, but he knew as he stared into this woman's eyes that time was running out.

"Save him," she spluttered. "Save him. Pl... please..."

That's when the smoke swallowed the cabin up.

The pair of them disappeared.

And all Max could hear was that baby's cry.

CHAPTER FOURTEEN

Aoife saw the flames inside the bus growing, and she knew there was no more time for calmness.

She had to get the hell out of here.

Fast.

She pushed against Harry's body, which pinned her down. He was heavy. So much heavier than he looked. Bastard. She didn't like the guy in the first place. Obviously wouldn't wish anything like this on him. But she'd seen the look in his eyes before the bus crashed. That look of total detestation after she rejected him. Something made her think that he'd be staring down on her now, smiling at the fact that he'd had the last laugh after all.

But she couldn't think like that. Right now, there was one thing on her mind.

She had to get out of this bus. Whether she was injured or not, and whether she did herself more damage or not. She couldn't wait around here for help anymore. She'd waited long enough, and it didn't seem like anyone was coming to her aid, for whatever reason.

So she had to help herself.

She saw herself as a child. Saw herself deep in the woods with her dad. Freezing cold. She heard him telling her that at some point in her life, she'd be alone. Whether physically or mentally, she'd feel cornered. And she'd be forced to work her way out of it, alone.

And whether it was physical or mental, the way of conquering any challenge was always the same.

Break down the task into smaller parts.

Focus on it pragmatically. One step at a time.

And do not lose your shit.

She took a deep breath. But that was a mistake right away because the smoke was already filling the bus. She looked around, her neck sore. Saw the opening at what was now the top of the bus, where the window was. She couldn't tell from here if the glass was smashed or not, but she just had to hope it was. Because if it wasn't...

No. Don't get ahead of yourself. One step at a time, like Dad always said.

She closed her eyes and focused on the one task before her that she knew she needed to conquer before anything else.

And that was getting free of Harry's body.

He was heavy, so it wasn't going to be easy. Far heavier than her. Pinning her down to the point she could barely breathe, and breathing wasn't an easy task anyway right now.

She tightened her fists. It was going to be tough. But she was going to have to use all the strength she had to get out of this.

She felt pinned down. Trapped. She didn't know she had the strength to get out of this.

But she just had to focus on getting from underneath Harry.

And then she had to worry about the next step.

Couldn't let the fire freeze her in her tracks before she'd even given herself a chance of getting out.

She tried to push herself up first. But she couldn't do that. Not only because of Harry's weight but also because of the pain she was feeling. The tightness in her back. Across her chest. And the dizziness she felt. Fuck. The last thing she wanted was to pass out right now. At least she had to give herself a chance of escaping.

Come on, Aoife. One step at a time. You've got this.

She decided not to even attempt pushing herself free of Harry again. It was useless. The only way she was getting from underneath him was if she wormed her way free. She remembered being a kid and getting stuck in some caves on a school trip. The fear she felt. And hearing the words her instructor shouted down to her.

Act like you're a worm! Use your whole body, every single muscle, and worm your way free!

She heard those words now and felt that same terror she'd felt back then, all those years ago.

And then she began worming her way backwards. Dragging herself from underneath Harry's weight.

Step by step by step.

All the time, the smell of smoke grew stronger.

The heat from the flames got warmer.

And Aoife's heart beat harder and harder and harder.

She dragged herself backwards. And in a moment of terror, she got an image of stretching her neck and Harry's weight falling down onto her, choking her to death, right before she burned—

No.

Don't think about that.

Just focus on getting out from under him.

She pulled herself back, more and more. And as the flames grew stronger, she thought about the emergency services again. Why weren't they here? Why was nobody here to help her?

And then she remembered her dad's words.

You can't always rely on other people to help you out, Aoife. Sometimes in life, you've got to find the strength to help yourself.

She closed her tearful eyes and yanked herself further out when she felt a burning pain right in her shin.

"Agh!"

She yelled out. Cried. Pulled back a little haphazardly, shifting Harry's weight more than she would've liked.

There was something in her leg.

Something sharp.

She needed to get it out.

She needed...

Aoife. One step at a time. One frigging step at a time.

She took a breath, even though the pain in her leg was immense.

She dragged herself further from under Harry.

Almost there. Almost...

And then she pulled herself free of Harry, who fell to the broken window of the bus again.

She stood up, dizzy, and keeled over straight away. The pain in her leg was bad. She looked down and saw a piece of glass sticking right out of her thigh.

Felt nauseous and sick, straight away. Went shivery and cold, even though it was getting hot in here.

She took a few deep breaths.

There was no time to wait.

No time to hesitate.

She yanked that shard of glass from her leg.

Blood trickled out.

She'd bandage it up as soon as she got away.

Right now, she needed to get out of here.

She needed to escape.

She looked up at the windows above. She couldn't see any smoke escaping out the top of them. So they weren't smashed by the looks of things.

Which meant she'd have to smash them first.

She looked around for something she could use. Anything.

And as the smoke got thicker, as she had to stop her breathing to stop herself choking, she saw a fire extinguisher at the back of the bus.

She limped over towards it.

Grabbed it.

Tried to shoot it towards the flames, but it spluttered and failed.

Damned public service cuts. Typical.

She looked up at the window above.

She'd need to balance on the side of one of the seats. She'd need to climb. And then she'd need to jump.

She shivered. Shook as she scrambled around to get on the edge of one of the chairs. She couldn't think anymore. She couldn't ponder. She just had to *act*.

She climbed onto the side of a chair, putting all the weight on her right side, and wished she'd stuck with those yoga classes to give herself some more flexibility and balance.

She pulled back the extinguisher.

She went to smash it against the glass.

And then she slipped off and fell and hit the floor.

She looked at the fire. It was spreading fast, covering the entire front of the bus now. No chance of getting out the door. She had to get out of a window. It was going to be her only way out.

But she couldn't. Not with this wound on her leg.

She looked at the piece of glass.

And then she looked up at the glass of the bus window again.

She looked up at it, and she broke the problems down into smaller ones, just as Dad would've told her to.

Think, Aoife. Think.

She gripped the extinguisher, tight in her hands.

She pulled back her arms.

"Here goes nothing," she said.

And then, as hard as she could, she threw it up towards the window.

A crack.

It fell back down beside her.

And even though the window hadn't smashed in the dramatic fashion she'd hoped, it was enough.

Enough for her to work with.

She climbed onto the chairs again. Winced with the agony in her left thigh.

And then she stretched out for the window, fire extinguisher balanced in her hands.

"Come on," she said, bashing against it. The smoke filling the bus now. So much so she felt dizzy. On the verge of collapse. "Please. Come on. Come…"

It all happened so fast.

The window broke.

The smoke escaped outside.

Glass rained down on Aoife.

She had a chance.

She reached up, stretched as far as she could, so far her fingers felt like they were going to pop out of her hands, her hands out of her arms, her arms out of their sockets.

Come on. Come on!

And then she felt the sharp broken glass at the edge of the broken bus window dig right into her palms, and despite the pain, she felt relief.

Total relief.

"Almost there. You can do this. Almost there."

She stretched. Pulled herself up. Even though she was sore, stiff, purely acting on adrenaline, she pulled.

She knew she could do this.

She knew she was strong enough.

She…

That's when she heard it.

A cough.

A cough from inside the bus.

She looked around. Frowned.

And then, in the glow of the flames, she saw something that made the hairs on the back of her neck stand right on end.

Harry's eyes were open.

He was lying there.

And he was alive.

He looked right up at her, terror in his eyes.

"Please," he whimpered. "Don't leave me. Help me. Please!"

CHAPTER FIFTEEN

Max watched the smoke fill the train cabin, drowning the mother from sight, and listened to the baby's screams.

It was boiling hot here. He was absolutely dripping with sweat. Seriously, it was really fucking hard to believe it was *actually* the middle of winter when he felt like he was standing in a furnace.

In front of him, a burning train. The train that had crashed when the power went out.

A lot of people had managed to crawl their way out of the train. Further down, though, Max saw a man dangling out of a window, half-burned. His stomach ripped apart from the window's jagged edges, digging into his torso. A woman screaming as she held her limp, burned child in her arms.

And behind, down on the ground, chaos. Panic. Pandemonium.

A realisation that this wasn't ordinary. That something very, very wrong was happening here.

And still there were no emergency services here to help.

Max turned back around. Looked at that smoking mass inside

the train's cabin. He could still hear that baby inside, crying away. No sign of the baby's mother anymore.

He knew what the logical thing to do would be. To turn away. To get the hell away from this train and get back home, where he'd be safe. Because he had supplies. He had gadgets, that if this were some kind of electromagnetic pulse or coronal mass ejection, would be protected from the fallout.

And most importantly, he didn't have any responsibilities. Didn't have anyone waiting on him.

And he preferred it that way.

But standing here, he knew he couldn't just let that be the case.

He knew he couldn't just give up on this woman and her child.

He pulled back his bloodied fists once more and smacked hard against the boiling hot glass.

It was hot. So hot. So hot that he had to stop immediately. He wasn't making any progress.

But the thought of turning away. The thought of giving up. The thought of letting this child die...

"No," he said.

He looked around. Saw that window the bloke had died trying to get out of. Could he get in through there? Did he have a chance?

He gritted his teeth. Heard debris tumble from the burning train somewhere behind him. Heard the lines creaking.

And in that moment of adrenaline, one thought came to mind.

"Fuck it," he said.

He rushed over to the glass. Saw the bloke dangling out of that train window. No wonder he'd hurt himself. Impaled himself on a real sharp piece of glass, by the looks of things.

And Max felt bad. Of course, he felt bad. He knew this guy probably deserved better than to be used as protection from the broken glass.

But right now, he needed to act fast.

He clambered his way inside and was hit with the double assault of thick, suffocating smoke and intense heat right away.

He tumbled against the floor of the train. The whole place felt like it was on fire. He could see the inferno over to his left. And he turned away from it immediately. He didn't want to see it. Didn't want to face it. Didn't want to accept that it was there, and it was real, and it was coming for him, and that he needed to get away from it—fast.

He covered his mouth as he spluttered. As the smoke stung his eyes, making him cry scorching hot tears. He squinted over towards where he'd seen the woman, heard the child, but he couldn't see anything for the smoke. Not a thing.

He stumbled forward. He wasn't even sure he was going in the right direction anymore. Wasn't sure about anything.

Only that he couldn't give up.

He had to keep trying.

Please, Max. Save him. Save David.

He heard her voice and took a few more steps forward. Bumped into a body lying there, unconscious. A man. Heard screaming down the carriage.

And all this time, he couldn't shift his attention from where he thought the woman was.

Where he thought her baby was.

And all this time…

He couldn't help noticing he couldn't hear the baby anymore.

He stood there. Shaking, even though he was roasting. His vision was fading. His body felt weak. If he stayed in here much longer, he was going to cough his guts up and die.

He had to walk away.

He had to go.

You failed. You failed, again.

"No!"

He stepped forward, and he saw her.

The woman.

The baby in her arms.

Both of them silent.

Both of them with their eyes closed.

Both of them gone.

He stood there in the burning inferno as the smoke picked up and stared at the pair of them.

And then, in that instant, he saw himself back at the house, three years ago.

Kathryn dying.

Going into the bedroom.

Finding David.

The pain he'd felt.

The grief he'd felt.

The anger at how he couldn't have done more.

He stood there and stared at the pair of these bodies as the smoke got thicker and the flames got closer, and he knew he didn't have a choice anymore.

So he turned around, staggered away, and climbed back out of that window.

Out into the air.

Out into the open.

Out into the darkness outside.

It was only when he'd staggered away from the train, down the steps, back to the ground, past all the panicking people, that he swore he heard a baby crying from inside that train.

CHAPTER SIXTEEN

"Please," Harry shouted. "Don't leave me here. Don't let me die here. Please!"

Aoife didn't know what the hell what happening or what the hell to do. Harry. He was alive. She was convinced he was dead. She'd wormed her way from underneath his heavy body, clambered her way across the bus, struggled to escape the smashed window, and dragged herself up it. Got a piece of glass in her leg for her troubles.

But this was supposed to be straightforward, now. There weren't supposed to be any more twists here. Any more turns. She was supposed to climb out of this bus and get away before the flames engulfed it. And then she was going to find help. Find someone who could help her. Help she was convinced should've already arrived by now.

But Harry.

She saw him crouched there amid the flames. Saw the sweat pooling down his face. Saw the tears interlinked with blood. And she felt so bad for him. Because sure, he was a shit to her. Sure, he was a creep. But his life was in danger here. The flames were growing around the bus. If she didn't help him out of here, he was going to be burned alive.

"Please. I'm sorry. I didn't—I didn't mean to hurt you. Just... My leg. It's stuck. Don't leave me here to die. Please."

She saw him struggling with his right leg, which was wedged between the chair and the side of the bus. And again, she sympathised. Because as much as she wanted to go back to him, as much as she wanted to help... she knew there wasn't much she could do for him. She wouldn't be able to drag him the way she'd escaped through. And those flames were getting thicker. The smoke was getting thicker. Time was running out.

In the end, she only had one choice.'

"I'm going to get help."

Harry's eyes widened. He looked like he was crying. "What? No. Don't leave me. Please don't leave me."

"There's—there's nothing I can do. But time's running out. I... I need to get help. I need to get us help and—and I will. I'll get help right now, and I'll get you out of there. I promise. I promise."

She saw him shaking his head.

Saw that wall of flames growing even brighter behind him.

It'd swallow him up in no time.

"No," he shouted. "Don't leave me. Don't leave me!"

She turned around and climbed off the side of the bus.

She was shaking. In shock, for sure. She felt cold. Freezing cold. Shivering. Everything looked... surreal. Everything shimmered like she was in some kind of dream. Some kind of nightmare.

Maybe that's what this was. A nightmare. She'd had vivid dreams before, dreams where she was being hunted, dreams she was being torn apart.

But nothing as vivid as this.

She looked around at her surroundings.

The bus had collided with a row of terraced houses. The front of it looked like it'd smashed through a tree, too. There were people on the streets. A baby crying somewhere.

And everything was so *dark*.

All of the street lamps were off.

All of the lights in the houses were off, too.

She wondered if the bus had hit something. If it'd damaged the electricity cables down here, caused a power cut.

But shit. She didn't have time to speculate.

Not while Harry was still shouting out for help in that burning bus.

"Help," she said, limping along.

A man looked around at her. He was standing by the side of his car, trying to work his phone. He looked at her with wide eyes. Inside the car, an old lady who looked... shit. She looked dead.

"Sorry," he said. "We all need help, love."

Aoife turned away from him, walked further down the road, towards the terraced houses. She could see a few people gathered by the houses. All of them looking at their phones. Trying to get their phones to work.

"There's—there's somebody in there," she shouted. "There's—there's a man in there. He's trapped. I got out, but he needs help. It's burning. Please!"

She saw these people staring at her. People asking her to sit down, to breathe. Telling her everything was going to be okay, but nothing could be done.

"The phones," a woman said. "The phones are all out. The power's all out. And even the cars are out, too. We can't get an ambulance down 'ere 'cause we can't let 'um know."

And Aoife didn't understand. She didn't get it. Only this whole scene was taking on the form of a nightmare more and more by the second.

She looked around at that burning bus. Her teeth chattered together. She could still hear shouting in there. Shouting, which got more and more pained by the second.

And as she watched the flames rise, she wanted to go back over there.

Because for all the shit Harry had put her through tonight... he was human.

He was afraid.

And he was alone.

She went to walk back, determined to help him however she could, when she heard a few shouts behind her.

Saw people running past.

Fear on their faces.

All looking up at the sky.

She turned around. Looked up.

That's when she saw it.

It was only small. But there was this light. This bright orange light, that looked like it was getting bigger and bigger.

"It's a plane!" someone shouted, running past her. "It's gonna blow the whole street up. Run!"

Aoife didn't get it. She didn't understand. She couldn't put two and two together.

But then, as that light grew brighter, and as a sound of something whizzing through the air grew in intensity, she realised, and her stomach dropped.

A plane.

There was a plane falling from the sky.

Hurtling to the ground.

And it was flying right towards her.

Fast.

CHAPTER SEVENTEEN

Max walked through the city centre and saw all the signs that this wasn't just as bad as he first feared—it was worse.

It was pitch black, and it was freezing cold. He didn't know exactly what time it was anymore because no phones were working. His watch wasn't working. Nothing at all was working.

It didn't matter, though. Not really.

What mattered was the events unfolding all around him.

He saw cars, completely stationary. People trying to get their phones to work, as much as they could see, everyone else was in the same boat. He could see burning. Flames. Smoke. And he could hear lots of shouting, too. Lots of screaming.

Somewhere in the distance, he heard a bang. A real earth-shattering bang. He'd seen something hurtling towards Earth. Thought it was a meteor at first. But it wasn't. It was a plane. A burning plane, crashing down towards Earth.

And all the signs were there. Signs he didn't want to accept. Didn't want to face.

But signs he couldn't run away from.

This was an EMP event.

He kept his head down as he walked down the street. His heart raced. He didn't even bother getting his car. It was an older Land Rover, but not old enough that it wasn't computerised, so it would be fried. Older cars would probably survive an electromagnetic pulse. He had another car in the garage that was mostly his hobby car, so he could give that a test when he got back.

But right now, in the city, a car was useless anyway.

He saw the chaos and disorder.

Burning buildings.

Screaming people.

He saw pockets of police trying to get the situation under control but failing to do so. Because they were frightened, too. They were scared, too.

They didn't know what the hell was going on either.

And it was only going to get all the more chaotic and confusing as the day went on.

He swallowed a lump in his throat. He'd read about the potential impacts of an EMP event a long time ago or a coronal mass ejection from the sun. There'd been plenty of CMEs throughout history. The most notable one that actually hit was the Carrington Event in 1859. A powerful coronal mass ejection hit Earth's magnetosphere and caused the biggest geomagnetic storm ever recorded.

Auroras were visible globally. They were so bright in the Rocky Mountains that they actually woke up the miners, who thought it was the rising sun. Telegraph systems all over Europe and North America were fried, some of them giving operators nasty and sometimes fatal electric shocks.

A solar storm of a similar scale today was always tipped to cause widespread, mass disruptions. The closest near miss was in 2012 when a solar storm narrowly missed.

But those lights. The talk of the lights.

Lights like the ones Max and the citizens of Preston had seen this evening.

He remembered the rumours of an oncoming solar storm he'd heard and how little attention he'd paid to the news. The news was always sensationalist. Over the last few years, Max's faith in mainstream media had plummeted. Preferred to live his own life without worrying about what he was told to do, about being scare-mongered by forces with their own intentions and motives.

But this... it seemed weird that it'd occurred, right on midnight.

It made him wonder if this was some sort of attack.

Some sort of coordinated attack made to look like it was a solar flare.

There were plenty of countries capable of exploding an EMP device. Both allies and enemies. And the impacts of a foreign aggressor getting an EMP in their hands was devastating.

First, the initial wave of deaths. Planes falling from the skies, 5,000 over America alone—and that was just America. Two million passengers dead in an instant, and not including the poor sods on the ground beneath them. Hospitals unable to operate, and ICU units wiped out in an instant. Cars slamming against one another. People with pacemakers in particularly strong blasts, dropping dead in an instant.

And then there were the longer tail problems. The looting, which would start pretty quickly. The stockpiling and the violence the battles for supplies would cause. An inevitable attempt at a military coup to maintain control and the disorder that would prompt.

The strongest surviving. The weakest dying.

Survival of the fittest gone mad.

Max swallowed a lump in his throat as he continued to walk. As much as he saw all the signs around him, he still clung to the belief that this would resolve. That it wouldn't play out like fiction predicted. Or like the experts predicted.

That humanity wouldn't lose its shit.

But he saw the panic already. The panic of being cut off from social media and from the news.

He saw the severed chains of connection crawling behind everyone's throats.

And it scared him.

He looked back at the city. Looked at the fire over by the train station. Looked at the smoke.

He thought of that child.

The baby in its mother's arms.

Finding them both lying there in the smoke.

Leaving the train, then hearing the cries.

And then he thought of David.

Help him, Max. Save him. Please.

Rushing into the bedroom.

Finding him with the knife to his throat.

And...

He gritted his teeth.

Tensed his jaw.

Kathryn was gone.

David was gone.

There was nothing he could do to save them now.

There was nothing he could do to save *anyone* now.

He looked at the rising smoke once more.

Then he took a deep breath, tensed his fists, and walked.

He had to get home.

He had to get the hell out of the city.

He had to get to safety.

And he had to do it alone.

CHAPTER EIGHTEEN

Aoife saw the plane hurtling towards the street, and she knew she had to get the hell away from here.

Fast.

She saw people running past her, tumbling in the road. She heard shouting. Screaming. People banging on doors, urging their neighbours to get out and get away. She heard children crying. Heard people protesting, not wanting to leave.

But all that time, the fireball got closer.

Closer and closer and—

She heard the shout from the bus, clear as day.

"Help! Help me! Don't leave me! Please!"

She heard that voice and right away, she knew it was Harry. And she wanted to go back there. She wanted to help him. Or at the very least, be with him in his final moments.

Because that's what they were.

That's what she had to face up to.

By walking away here, she was condemning Harry to death.

She felt someone bump into her. A man holding his daughter, who screamed, racing away. The fear in the eyes of these people as they faced up to the reality that soon, they wouldn't have a home.

Aoife didn't know what was happening. She didn't understand any of it.

But she knew one thing for sure.

She had to get off this street.

She had to go.

She'd done everything she could.

She looked back at that plane.

And she could *clearly* see it was a plane, now.

Hurtling closer and closer with speed.

She gritted her teeth and turned around.

And then, with all the strength she had in her body and being carried by adrenaline alone, she ran.

Her leg hurt. Not as bad as she'd expected, but bad enough that it slowed her down considerably. At least it wasn't bleeding as bad as she was expecting it to. That was something. A small victory.

She wanted to stop by the bus. She wanted to check on Harry. She wanted to make sure he was okay.

But she didn't have time.

She didn't have time at all.

And she didn't want to look at the bus.

She didn't want to see.

She didn't want to accept that she was leaving him here.

She was condemning him to his death.

She felt the heat from the bus. And inside there, she thought she could hear someone crying.

"Please, Mum. Please."

And that whimpering broke her.

That childish innocence broke her.

Because as horrible as he'd been to her, and as bad a guy as he seemed... he didn't deserve this.

Nobody deserved this.

She looked back around.

Wondered if there was time to act.

And then she saw that plane getting closer, too close for comfort, and she knew her time was up.

"I'm sorry," she said. "I'm so sorry."

She looked away from the bus, and at that moment, that instant, she focused on one thing and one thing only.

Running.

She ran. Ran as fast as she could, as fast as her sore leg would allow. She wasn't going as fast as she could, but far faster than she should be able to, courtesy of the adrenaline.

She knew she'd be doing some damage. She knew she was only going to make the sore leg even worse.

But a sore leg wasn't a bad thing when there was a fucking plane hurtling towards the street.

She saw people alongside her, running for their lives, like a flock of sheep fleeing wolves.

She heard the cries and the shouts. Watched people tumble over, then clamber back to their feet.

She looked around.

Saw it getting closer—

Tripped.

Slammed against the road, cutting her hands.

"Fuck."

She pushed herself up, heart racing. Steadied herself. Then she ran again. She figured there wasn't long left. That plane was getting far closer, far faster than she was expecting.

She had to keep running.

She had to keep...

She saw her, then. A girl lying on the road. Her ankle looked like it'd cocked over.

She saw her, and she knew she had to help.

She couldn't just leave her.

Couldn't just run past her.

Not like everyone else.

She ran over to her. "Here," she said. "Take my arm. Quick."

The girl shook her head. "My ankle. It's so sore—"

"It'll be a whole lot sorer if you don't take my hand right this second."

The girl nodded. Grabbed onto her.

"Right," Aoife said. "This might hurt."

And then she dragged her to her feet.

The girl screamed with pain. But she ran. She ran with Aoife as Aoife dragged her along. And Aoife held on to her. Held onto her for dear life. Because she wasn't going to let someone else go. Wasn't going to let someone else die.

No.

You did everything you could for him.

Everything.

She ran further and further. She could hear the plane getting closer like it was tearing through the atmosphere. Everything felt hotter. Like she was in an inferno.

"It's getting closer," the girl cried.

"Focus ahead," Aoife said.

"But—"

"Just focus ahead."

She focused on the road ahead.

Dropped into her mindfulness practice as best as she could.

Let adrenaline carry her along.

Kept going.

Kept running.

She always kept going in times of trauma. In times of pain.

She had to just keep on putting one foot in front of the other, and—

It all happened in slow motion.

First, losing her footing.

Tumbling to the road.

The girl beside her falling with her.

And then, right behind her, a crash.

And an almighty blast.

CHAPTER NINETEEN

Seth knew something was wrong the moment the lights went out.

It was crazy in here. Everyone was losing their fucking minds. He could hear them shouting, banging on the doors of their cells, screaming out. Always the way when there was a power cut. Lunatics, that's what they were. Lunatics and savages. He was glad to be away from them, stuck in solitary confinement. Only way he could get a minute's peace in this place.

But there was something he noticed when those lights went out that made him think that perhaps something, well, *different,* was going on here.

It was the lack of alarm. Weird thing to notice, sure, the lack of something. But it struck him right away. When there'd been power cuts in the past, the lights usually went out briefly, and an alarm sounded, loud as hell.

But right now, Seth didn't hear a thing. Nothing but the shouting of the inmates. Banging against their cell doors. And the shouting of the prison guards, getting louder, louder, louder...

And it made him wonder.

Was something different here?

Was something truly wrong?

He sat on his bed, which wasn't exactly Ritz quality, but it was comfortable enough. Probably more comfortable than he deserved, after all. He'd done some horrible things in his life. He wasn't going to sit here and pretend he'd been hard done by. He really had done some nasty shit. Burglaries. Robberies. Beaten more people up than he could remember. Tortured a fair few people, too, some unnecessarily.

But the crime he was in for...

Shit.

He smirked when he thought of it.

When he thought of her screams.

When he thought of his little sleeping face.

And then the look in the eyes of the husband when he came back in, desperate as anything.

Seth shook his head. He knew he should *feel* bad about what he'd done. But at the end of the day, he didn't really *feel* much. He'd accepted he wasn't quite screwed up right, up in the head, a long, long time ago. As a child, he started pulling the legs off insects and watching them stumble along, so determined to escape, to survive. He once pulled all the legs off a spider and was fascinated by how it just sat there, trapped in its own little body. He kept it for a while. He was never sure whether it was alive or dead, but he'd throw flies in there for it, just to give it a chance.

Just so he could keep it longer.

He remembered the first time he'd stepped up to killing a cat. It was a stray. One he saw wandering along the street. Nudged up against his leg. He remembered the feeling of power he felt. The feeling of complete control. The way the cat trusted him. How it saw something *good* in him.

And then picking it up and breaking its neck in one fell swoop.

The poor little thing never knew what hit it.

So he guessed it was only natural he'd ended up murdering

somebody. Two people, in fact. Although he'd never planned on "graduating" to people. Mostly it was for revenge. Revenge against the guy who took everything away from him, right when his life was going so, so well...

He thought of the look on the man's face as he stood there in his son's bedroom. The panic and the horror and the grief.

And it reminded him of that spider all those years ago. Trapped.

He heard more shouting up above, in the main cell area. Still no alarms. But it sounded like shit was really hitting the fan. Like there was rioting going on up there. Primates, they were. Scumbags with barely a brain cell between the lot of them.

But Seth was different. He was intelligent. Sure, he hadn't exactly achieved much in life. But that's because he saw what a cacophony of bullshit playing the game of life really was when you really thought about it.

Why spend life living by somebody else's rules? Why follow the boring, inane path of capitalism, of commuting, of a hamster wheel to a retirement you're probably not gonna enjoy anyway because you'll end up contracting some rare form of cancer probably attributed to the years of stress you've faced working for somebody else? For the years spreading your arse cheeks and being fucked by the system, repeatedly, right to your grave?

Why do all that when you could just have fun and be, well, human?

Truly human?

Seth stepped up to his cell door. He listened to the shouting above. The bangs. Stood there in the darkness and breathed deeply. He'd dreamed of this moment. He didn't want to sound superstitious, but he had. He'd had dreams before that he'd woken up in the middle of a riot, all the lights out.

Walked over to his cell door.

Pushed against it, and...

Freedom.

Free as a bird.

And the best thing?

The world was a playground out there for him.

As soon as he finished what he had to do.

As soon as he concluded the business he'd started, three long years ago.

He lifted a hand. Realised he was shaking. Because this felt just like the dreams he'd had. This felt so real. To the point he wondered if this *was* a dream.

There was only one way to find out.

He put his hand against his cell door.

He swallowed a lump in his throat.

And then, expecting nothing, but excited nonetheless, he pushed.

The door swung open.

The corridor to solitary confinement was empty.

He stared out at that corridor, and a smile stretched across his face.

A smile that grew wider when he thought about the woman, Kathryn.

The boy, David.

Killing the boy and stabbing her.

All in revenge for what her husband, for what the boy's father, took from him.

He thought of the husband—thought of Max, the police officer who ruined his life—and he smiled.

Seth's work wasn't finished.

He took a deep breath, stepped out into the corridor, into the darkness.

Then, free as a bird, he flew.

He had unfinished business to attend to.

CHAPTER TWENTY

Aoife slammed against the road and heard the enormous blast erupt behind her.

For a moment, night became day. The darkest, blackest night she'd ever encountered, suddenly illuminated to levels of brightness she'd never before witnessed. Her ears rang and rang, and it felt like they were going to burst, to explode. She wasn't sure if she was in pain or not. She couldn't tell. She'd lost all sense of her body, of her surroundings.

She just felt this intense heat and this brightness, and for a moment, just a moment, everything just stood still.

And then she blinked a few times, and her vision started to return.

She was holding onto somebody's hand. All around her, she could see people running away. But some people hadn't got away. People were lying on the burning street around her. Bricks flying from houses; chunks of metal flying past and slamming into people, knocking them to the road.

There were dying people. Dead people. And even though her ears were ringing so loud that she couldn't hear anything else, she could see the screams of people covered in blood. Or people missing arms. Or legs.

She looked around at this scene of horror as her vision started to return even stronger, as the ringing in her ears faded, just slightly, and then she looked at its source.

Up ahead, almost unbearably bright to look at, there was a plane. Burning out. Torn to shreds.

By its side, houses. Houses that were now exploding. Bricks exploding everywhere, like fireworks. Landing in the street, some of them on people on that street.

And there were body parts.

Bodies.

She saw people running through the flames, the flames clawing through their clothes and skin.

She saw the tears in their eyes. The horror on their faces.

She saw their screams as they tried to clutch to chunks of their disintegrating flesh before falling to the road in a heap.

She saw it all happening, smelled the burning meat in the air, heard the crying and screaming, and beyond this light, the total, black darkness, and she wanted to get away from here. She wanted to turn away and run.

But she was frozen.

Completely frozen.

She saw the spot where the bus was, then. Or at least, where she thought the bus was. The one she'd escaped. The one Harry had been trapped in.

And as she looked at it, her teeth chattered together. Because that could have been her in there. She could've woken up later and not known a thing about it. Or woken up just slightly too late.

Or woken up to Harry leaving her.

Being left alone and afraid.

He was gone now. There was no coming back from that kind of disaster.

But the pain she felt. The pain at the sense of responsibility she had...

She felt the hand in hers. The hand of the girl she'd saved. At least she'd saved someone's life. At least she'd done one good deed.

But when she turned around, she noticed something.

The girl wasn't holding her hand.

There *was* a hand there.

But there was nobody attached to it.

Aoife let out a cry, dropped the arm.

She looked around.

Saw a girl lying there.

A girl just like the one she'd saved.

A chunk of metal debris in her skull.

Eyes wide open.

Blood pouring from her lips.

Missing an arm, torn away by the wreckage.

Aoife could barely breathe. She felt dizzy. Sick.

But when she heard the next explosion, when she saw more chunks of brick falling down, she knew there was no time to stand around here.

She had to get away.

Had to stay alert.

She couldn't go collapsing or passing out.

She was lucky to be here in the first place.

Now, she had to get away.

She stumbled down the street. She couldn't run anymore. She was shaking. The shock. The adrenaline. All of it.

She looked around at the dead bodies. Smelled them. That's the worst part. That smell of burning. And how, in a stomach-turning sort of way, it actually reminded her of the smells of a summer barbecue.

A smell she'd never be able to enjoy again.

She walked further, shakily, down the street.

There was nobody here.

No ambulances.

No police.

Nobody.

And as much as she wanted to believe someone would come to her aid, she couldn't shake that feeling that this was bigger than even the police.

All the power out.

All the phones out.

And planes falling from the skies.

Whatever this was... it was big.

She looked around. Looked at the bodies. Looked at the people who were beyond saving.

Looked at people running away.

She looked at the fire. At the burning. At the destroyed terraced houses, at the decimated plane.

At the entire scene of destruction.

She looked at it all, and she knew there was no use staying here.

She looked at the spot where the bus was one final time.

I'm sorry, Harry. I'm sorry.

Then she wiped a tear away, and without any direction in mind, she walked.

CHAPTER TWENTY-ONE

Max saw the convenience store in the distance, and he had an idea.

It was late. The pitch-black hadn't eased one bit. He'd been walking for what felt like forever now, and everywhere he walked, he saw the same sights. No lights. No power. Smatterings of chaos and destruction all around. He saw cars completely stationary. People sat in some of them, hands against the steering wheels like they were waiting for some invisible force to swoop in and save them. A force that wasn't coming.

Other cars were abandoned. Max grunted. At least those people had the right idea. Best thing to do right now was get away from any populated areas. To get the hell to the rural areas. Well. The best thing to do was to *be* there already.

But Max just happened to be working on the night the power went out. The night every frigging thing went to shit.

Just typical.

He knew he should get back as quickly as possible, especially after the huge blast he'd heard not long ago, but he was standing outside the convenience store just outside the city, and he knew there were things he was short on back home. He knew there were things he needed. Supplies. Things he could do with stocking up on, saving himself a trip back into the city, giving him a head start and an opportunity to survive the first days in the wilderness...

Or, well. To ride this out for as long as it lasted, anyway. He had to stop thinking in terms of worst-case scenarios. He had to stop thinking in absolutes. He had to just take this one step at a time.

And as it stood, he had an advantage. He had a head start.

He took a deep breath and stepped into the twenty-four-hour convenience store, which seemed weird in itself because it was so dark, because the lights were all out. One of those places attached to a petrol station. Not exactly ideal. Not a supermarket, or anything like that.

But it would do, for now.

He walked through the door. It was so dark. So eerie. There was nobody in here, and it didn't look like anybody had been here yet at all.

He had to take advantage of that. Had to make the most of that.

The first thing he headed towards was the cosmetics aisle. Dental floss. Not the first thing anyone would typically think to hoard in case of a disaster, but Max wasn't just anyone. He knew his stuff. Tales from the military. Years of research on survival. Really, you'd think he was in his element right now. A real opportunity to test his skills.

He already had a fully kitted out bug-out bag back at home, containing all the supplies he'd need if he was trapped out in the wilderness without power, forced to survive.

Just never imagined he'd ever actually need it.

But there were no thoughts like that in his mind.

Just a pure survival mentality.

Dental floss was handy because it had multiple purposes, and yet it was something most people looked past entirely. Set aside the fact that oral health would be all the more important in a world where it wasn't as easy to look after yourself, and it had a whole bunch of other handy purposes, too.

It could be used to create DIY stitches, perfect for emergencies. Or to make a fishing line. Really, the possibilities were endless.

Max knew another few uses for floss, too. You could turn a knife into a spear by tying it to a branch. You could wrap it around tree trunks, use it to trip an enemy, an almost invisible tripwire. And it could be utilised in animal traps, too.

He hoped he wouldn't have to go too far down those routes, though.

But he had to be prepared.

There were a few other things he grabbed, too. Jars of peanut butter. The perfect food, in a way. Packed with protein. Combined with crackers, went a hell of a long way.

And sure. Max liked his food. And the thought of crackers and peanut butter as a main meal wasn't exactly the most appetising.

But it would do. It would suffice.

It would get him through.

He picked up some canned beans, some white rice, some tins of meat and vegetables, and a few energy bars. The sort of stuff he had at home, but you could never have too much of this stuff in a time of crisis.

There were a few other things he grabbed, too. More things he figured the average person wouldn't think of. Blankets. Candles. Lighters. A few painkillers and personal hygiene items, like soap, toothpaste, sanitiser.

And even water, too. Sure, he knew how to set a rain catchment system up. But that would take time. For now, a stockpile of water was going to be handy, especially with the sanitation crisis that the blackout was going to spur.

He took a deep breath as he stared at the supplies, all of

which he'd tucked into a rucksack off the shelf. More than he'd hoped to be lugging around with him. But it would do for now.

And for a moment, it hit him just how crazy this was.

Was he being excessive?

Over the top?

Kathryn would definitely have teased him for this once upon a time.

But then he sighed.

It looked serious out there. Better to be safe than sorry.

He walked over to the counter.

There was nobody here. Nobody at all.

He stood there a few seconds. Felt guilty. Because this was stealing. He read about the potential of looting when the world went to shit, and he felt bad about it. Uncomfortable about it. He didn't want to be one of those people.

But then, this was the new world. For however long it lasted... this was the new world. Like it or not.

He put the basket down anyway. Put his hands into his pocket to retrieve whatever cash he had in there.

And then he heard footsteps right behind him.

"Put that right down," someone said. "Put that right down and get the hell out of my shop. Now."

CHAPTER TWENTY-TWO

Aoife walked into the night and felt so, so lost.

It was late. She had no idea what time it was. Everywhere she walked, she kept on hoping she'd come across some new evidence that this was limited to a really local area. Or that the emergency services were on this, getting control of the situation.

Or just some *sign* that gave her a fragment of hope that this wasn't permanent. That this was temporary, and like everything temporary, it was going to be fixed, in time.

But she didn't see a thing like that.

She just kept on seeing reminders that the city was falling apart, and nobody was stepping in to save it.

She saw cars in the middle of the road. Some of them had crashed into one another. Others had just been abandoned. She smelled smoke in the air. Every now and then, she'd hear the sound of a shout or a cry. And it scared her. The whole thing scared her. Because it felt unpredictable. It felt like anything could happen. Like the shackles were off a lot of people, and they were running wild now.

She just kept her head down and walked. Cold. Shaking. Shivering with adrenaline and with the freezing cold of the air.

She had to get back to the flat.

She had to get back to...

Kayleigh.

Kayleigh and her flatmates.

She thought about them, and she felt guilty right away. So guilty. Because she hadn't spared a single thought for them since the accident. Hadn't thought where they might be or what they might be going through.

She thought of them in that nightclub, the lights going on. Or on the streets, watching the countdown, watching the confusion. Imagined their panic. Their fear.

Wherever they were, she hoped they were okay. Because even though she felt like she wasn't exactly on the same *plane* as them, when it came to life, they were still people, after all. And they were good people. Decent people. People with good hearts.

She hoped they were okay.

Wherever they were, she hoped they were okay.

She kept her head down and walked. Her leg was sore but not as bad as she'd first feared, especially now she'd wrapped it up. She was terrified; make no mistake about it. The things she'd been through. The things she'd witnessed. And the deaths she felt responsible for. She thought of Harry. She thought about the girl she'd been running along with when the plane crashed and exploded.

She thought of them both, and she wondered if she could've done more to help.

But she kept on going. Because as scared as she was, as terrified as she was, she'd faced adversity in the past, and she'd got through it. She'd had the rug pulled from under her feet so many times in life.

She thought about Jason. Her husband. How perfect he

seemed. How perfect *everything* seemed. How convinced she was that he was the guy she was going to grow old with. Her soulmate.

She remembered walking into the hotel bedroom that day when they were away in the Algarve on honeymoon.

She remembered what she saw...

And how her life changed in that instant.

She shook her head. She didn't want to think about that. She didn't want to revisit it. She'd thought about it enough times as it was. And the more she thought about it, it still never made any more sense.

She kept her head down and walked further down the street, focusing on footstep after footstep. *Bring your awareness to the present moment.* That's what she'd been taught. *Bring your awareness to the present, and everything will be good. Everything will be okay. All that exists is the present moment. Not the past. Not the future. Just the now.*

She focused on step after step after step when she heard something.

It was a dog. It sounded like it was close by somewhere. Barking.

She looked around. Her heart picking up. She'd had a dog when she'd lived with Jason. A little Jack Russell called, creatively, Jack. She'd always liked dogs. Always wanted one when she was younger, but Dad wasn't keen on the idea. Didn't see the point of unnecessary sentimental attachments. Held people back, that's what he said.

And when she was older, she'd always lived in flats that didn't allow pets, so she'd just never had the perfect opportunity. The perfect chance.

So hearing this dog now, for some reason—probably a mixture of the heightened emotions of everything—she looked around for it and felt like she wanted a companion.

She looked around, and she saw it.

It was in the front yard just ahead. A Rottweiler. Big dog. Really big. Had a mean bark. Really mean.

But it looked... weirdly sad.

Like it was trying to get out.

Aoife knew she should just keep walking. That it wasn't any of her business.

But she felt sorry for it, being out here in the cold, all alone.

So she walked over to it.

The houses it lived at were a bit rough. Not the nicest area in the city. Not the kind of people she wanted to get involved with.

But she got closer to it and saw it wagging its little docked tail.

"Hi," she said. Wanting companionship more than anything. Just wanting someone—something—to connect with on this loneliest of nights. "Are you okay?"

The dog stopped barking. Jumped down from the gate. Wagged its tail. Its ears were back. It looked timid. Shy.

"It's okay," Aoife said. "Don't worry. You're not on your own anymore."

She got closer to it, right to the gate, when she noticed something.

Something that made her heart sink.

The dog's back was lined with marks. Marks that were quite clearly burns.

Cigarette burns.

And she felt an anger at that moment. A rage at that moment.

Because whoever owned this dog clearly mistreated it.

Clearly didn't look after it.

And she wasn't sure if it was the change in circumstances. She wasn't sure if it was because of the adrenaline of everything that'd happened. She wasn't sure at all.

But Aoife found herself opening that gate.

Letting the dog out.

She expected the dog to go running off.

But it stayed there.

"Not want to go?" she asked.

The dog looked at her. Tongue dangling out. Tilting its head, side to side.

She smiled. "Go on. Time for you to go now."

She turned around and started walking when she heard the dog's nails against the road.

She looked around. Saw the dog was following. Keeping its distance but following.

She looked at it, and she smiled. Because if she just walked and the dog just followed, she wasn't stealing. Not technically. Right?

She looked at the dog and nodded her head. "Okay then," she said. "You can keep your distance. You can follow. We'll get used to each other eventually."

She turned around and walked.

Heard the dog's nails against the concrete.

And she didn't feel alone anymore.

She didn't feel lost anymore.

She felt more comfortable.

More reassured.

For the first time since the power went out, a smile stretched across Aoife's face.

That's when she heard a door slam open behind her.

When she heard footsteps racing down a path.

When she heard a shout.

"Oi! Come the fuck back here with my dog. Now!"

CHAPTER TWENTY-THREE

"Put everything you're carrying down right this second and get the hell out of my shop. Now."

Max heard the footsteps behind him and sighed. He should've known this was all too easy, all too good to be true. He'd come in here, found more supplies than he was even hoping to find, and he'd just been about to lay some money on the counter —out of guilt more than anything.

And now he was faced with the store's owner. Or the shopkeeper at least, seeing as this was one of those mini supermarkets on the side of a petrol station.

He turned around and saw the man standing there.

He was an Asian guy. Tall. Quite thin.

And he was holding something that made the hairs on Max's arms stand on end.

He had a machete in his hand.

"Come on," Max said. "There's no need for—"

"Don't you tell me what there's a need for when you're in my shop, stealing from me."

"Last time I checked, this wasn't your store," Max said, knowing full well he was pushing his luck a little. "It's a petrol station. Which means you have to take my money. And by the way, I wasn't stealing. I was going to leave some cash on the counter. Right here, see?"

The man stared through the darkness at Max. His nose twitched. And Max swore he heard movement on the other side of the shelves, too. Like someone was approaching that way. Ambushing him.

"Don't get cute with me," the man said. "You put that rucksack down, and you leave right now, and nobody needs to get hurt."

Max saw the man holding the machete, and he felt torn. Because, on the one hand, he knew he had to be careful. This man looked reckless. Crazy.

But on the other hand, he trusted his own instincts and his ability to fight. Even against a man wielding a machete.

"I've got the money," Max said. "Let me take these things and like you said. There doesn't need to be trouble."

"Money?" the man spat. "Don't give me that bullshit. You know as well as I do money's worthless, now. You've seen it out there. If you weren't at least somewhat smart about what's going on, you wouldn't be in here. You'd be out there panicking with everyone else. Biding your time, waiting for things to right themselves. But I've seen the sort of things you've picked off the shelves. I've seen the sort of supplies you've stuffed into that rucksack. You know what you're doing. Exactly what you're doing. So you'll know also that I'm deadly serious when I tell you to get the hell out of my shop and put my supplies down before you do. Right now."

Max had to admit he was impressed, at least slightly. Impressed but also pissed that he'd happened upon a store where the guy working clearly knew a thing or two about what he was talking about. It looked like he saw the significance of the power outage. Of just how widespread the ramifications could be and how things could get really nasty really fast.

But at the same time... he felt like there was only one solution here.

"It looks like we're at an impasse then, doesn't it?" Max said.

The man stayed still. Kept holding on to that machete. "Don't push your luck, mate. Don't try anything stupid. I'm warning you. If you take that stuff—"

"And the power comes right back on; how are you going to explain that?"

"Anything will be explainable," the man said. "But let's face it. We both know the power isn't coming on any time soon."

Again, the guy had a point. It would be very hard for the police to arrest anyone for any kind of crime committed in this world. It would all be too easily covered up. The guy could just drag Max's body outside and make it look like he'd died being hit by debris or anything.

And Max knew what the sensible option was here.

Put the stuff down.

Try another store.

But he wasn't one to walk away from conflict.

He took a deep breath, and he walked towards the man.

"I'm going to leave fifty quid on the counter. It's right there. Do with it what you want."

He kept walking.

"And I'm going to leave the store right now. You're not going to hurt me. You've got plenty here to get by. What I've taken isn't excessive. But you might want to gather what you need and get the hell out of the city before you find yourself in trouble."

He stopped, right before the man.

"I'm going to walk past you right now. And you're not going to do a thing. Okay?"

Max held eye contact with the guy.

Watched him search his face.

"I really didn't want to do this," the man said.

He pulled back his machete.

Went to swing it.

And Max flipped.

He pulled back his fist.

Buried it in the man's stomach.

Hard.

And then he grabbed his arm as the machete came flying down towards him.

Kneed him in the balls.

Headbutted him.

Twisted his arm until it cracked and then grabbed the machete from his loose hand as he cried out.

And then he sat over the man, machete raised in the air, and for a moment, he didn't see the shopkeeper at all.

For a moment, he saw the killer.

He saw Kathryn.

And he saw himself going into David's bedroom.

Finding him lying there in a pool of blood.

The killer standing there, smile on his face.

The anger and the pain and—

"Please!"

He heard that voice and looked down.

Back in the room again. Back in the store again.

The shopkeeper lying there beneath him, wincing, crying, tears in his eyes.

"Please," he said. "Just go. Just take it and go!"

And Max felt bad as he crouched with the machete over him. Because he was close. Close to burying that blade into his neck. Close to killing him.

Close to pouring all the rage he'd felt about his wife and son's death, all those years ago, into this man—this man who was just trying to defend what he thought was his.

Max lowered the machete. "I'm taking this too."

And then he stood up from the wincing man and rushed towards the door.

"Keep the money," Max said. "And get yourself away from here as quickly as you can. But a word of warning. Don't fuck with anyone like that again. You won't be so lucky next time."

Max turned around and stepped out of the store into the night.

That's when, just around the corner, he heard a woman's scream.

CHAPTER TWENTY-FOUR

"Come the fuck back with my dog right now!"

Aoife heard the shouts from the house, and she froze. Her heart raced. Adrenaline surged. Because this guy. He looked angry. Mad. And he looked like a piece of shit, too, to be quite frank.

Gangly. Skinny. Dark circles under his eyes. Pale face. Looked like a junkie.

"You think you can just walk into my yard and steal from me 'cause the lights are out, you posh bitch?"

"I didn't—"

"I saw you. I see people like you all the time. Looking down yer noses at us. Judging us. About time you were taught a lesson."

"I saw your dog barking," Aoife said, adrenaline surging, survival instincts taking hold. "I didn't know there was anybody home. I thought it needed help. So I let him free."

The guy shook his head. He was the kind of guy who couldn't be reasoned with; that much was for sure. His eyes, illuminating in the light of the moon, looked distant. Like he was high as a kite. He reeked of weed, too.

But the main thing that caught Aoife's attention was how the dog was acting.

It stood back. Cowered, ears turned back. Docked tail tucked in. And right by her side. Not in a hurry to get back to its owner. Which was what worried her. Because usually, a dog was loyal to its owner. So loyal, through all kinds of traumas.

But this dog looked like it didn't want to go anywhere near its owner.

"Rex?" the bloke said. "Come the fuck here right now."

But the dog—Rex—didn't budge. He just stood there. Tilted his head either side. Whined. Clearly not comfortable.

And now Aoife was closer to the dog she could see the markings on his back more.

The sores where some of his fur had been burned away, presumably by cigarettes.

The sight of his spine through his skin.

He looked mistreated. Malnourished.

And he definitely didn't look in a hurry to get back to his owner.

"Oi!" the man shouted. "Get the fuck back here. Now!"

And Aoife worried that his dog's reluctance was making things worse. Like the dog was insulting him, right before them both.

She watched as the dog, Rex, walked slowly back towards his owner.

Watched him, head lowered, eyes wide.

And she wondered what kind of a life he was going back to. What kind of hell he was going to face for daring to walk away, daring to abandon his owner.

She thought about it all when she felt a sudden strength.

She wasn't sure whether it was the adrenaline. She wasn't sure where it came from.

But it was that deep sense of strength inside her that made her stand up.

"He's coming with me," Aoife said.

The bloke stopped. Frowned. "You what? Why the fuck are you even still here?"

Aoife's heart raced. She didn't know what she was doing or why she was doing this, only that she had to do something. "The dog. Rex. He's clearly mistreated by you. And he clearly doesn't want to be with you. I'm—I'm not letting him go back with you."

The man smirked. Shook his head. "Oh yeah? And how do you plan on stopping me taking my own fucking dog back home, eh?"

She swallowed a lump in her throat.

"Rex?" she said. "Come here, boy."

Rex turned around in an instant.

His ears rose.

His little docked tail wagged.

And he ran over to Aoife's side.

She looked at the man standing there. Wide-eyed. His mouth moving, but no words coming out.

"Looks like he's made his choice," Aoife said.

She stood there with Rex by her side, and she felt a sense of panic creeping up inside. Because this guy. He'd been rejected. Rejected by his own dog. And truth be told, Aofie figured that would hurt him more than actually losing his dog. The fact he'd been embarrassed. Embarrassed by an outsider.

And that built Aoife's sense of urgency.

Her need to get the hell away from here.

Fast.

"If you don't mind," she said. "We're going to go now."

She turned around and went to walk when she felt a hand grab her hair and yank it back tight.

Instinctively, and something she wasn't proud of, she let out a cry.

The man tightened his grip on her hair and whispered into her ears with his sickly breath. "You're not going anywhere," he said.

CHAPTER TWENTY-FIVE

Max heard the shout from up the road, and he froze.

It was dark. Pitch black. The air was cold, but Max felt boiling hot. He had the machete in his hand, and he knew how ominous that would make him look, right in the middle of the street. He was still reeling a little from the stand-off with the guy working in the store. How close he'd been to burying the machete into his neck, to getting revenge for what happened to him three years ago, just on the wrong guy.

He thought he'd controlled his anger. Thought he'd managed it.

But he was starting to wonder if he'd just buried it, after all.

That shout. A woman. And the sound made him shiver. Because it made him think of how Kathryn must've shouted when the bloke stepped into their house that night when he was finishing work late.

The bloke he'd arrested a few times.

The bloke whose girlfriend he'd arrested.

The bloke who'd hunted his family down and killed them, and then smiled as Max stood over their bodies...

He heard that shout echoing around his skull, and he wanted to go and help.

But then he lowered his head and sighed.

He needed to get the hell away from here. He needed to get back home—fast. He'd already run into trouble in the store. Definitely didn't want to be taking any more chances.

He went to walk when he heard another shout.

He stopped.

That shout, it sounded just like Kathryn.

So much like her that it could be her.

He stood there, tensing his fists, shaking.

Just walk away, Max. Just walk away. It isn't your business to get involved in. It...

"Please," the woman shouted.

And that's what made Max turn around.

Please.

The same word Kathryn had said to him when she'd asked him to check on David.

When she'd begged him to save his life.

He heard that word, and he knew he couldn't walk away, not anymore.

He walked. Walked fast. And then he started running. A sense of urgency he couldn't even describe building up inside.

He knew he should turn away. He knew he should run. He knew he had no business getting involved in any of this.

But right now, he felt like he was on rails.

Like he had no choice.

Like instinct was driving him.

He reached the road where he'd heard the cry, and he saw a scene before him.

A woman was on her knees. A man was dragging her away. Beside them both, a dog, who looked a bit nervous about the whole endeavour.

"Come on," the bloke said, facing the other way, pulling her by her hair. "You're so keen on my dog then you can fucking come home with us."

The dog growled.

The man turned on it, spat at it. "And you're in deep shit, too, you little mutt."

The dog cowered, but then it followed.

And just watching this all transpire, Max once again felt that sense he shouldn't be here. That this wasn't his fight. That he was involving himself in unnecessary drama and should stay well away.

But then he saw the way this woman was struggling—fighting but struggling—and he knew he couldn't just walk.

"Leave her alone," Max said.

The man stopped. Turned around. Glared at him. The woman opened her eyes, still trying to fight her way through, not giving up.

"You what?" the man said.

Max stood there. Heart pounding. Machete in his sweaty palms. "I told you to leave her alone. And leave the dog alone, too. Clearly doesn't want to be anywhere near you."

The man let go of the woman. Tossed her to the road. He walked towards Max, laughing. "What the fuck is it with you people today? You got a death wish or something, buddy?"

"No," Max said. And then he did something he knew would be risky. He raised the machete. "But if you step a single step closer to me, you're in deep shit. Let her go. Let the dog go. And we'll be done here."

The man stopped for a moment. Shook his head.

And then he walked towards Max.

"See, I don't believe you," he said. "Not a posh fucker like you. I mean, you've got balls, I'll give you that. But I don't think you'd do a thing. None of you would. Not really. This bitch here, she tried to steal my dog. She's a stuck-up cow, and she'll pay for it."

"No," Max said, calmly as ever. "She won't. And I think the

dog's better off without you judging by the condition it's in, anyway."

The man stepped right up to Max. Shook his head.

"Not a step closer," Max said.

"Lower the machete, dickhead. Come on. Look at the size of you next to me. It's not like you need it, is it?"

Max figured the guy had a point.

He lowered the machete.

"Why can't we just have a conversation here?" the bloke said. "No need to get all fucking violent. You don't know the full story."

"I don't need to know the full story. I can see it with my own eyes."

"We're all in the shit. And this girl, whether you like it or not, she was stealing my dog. You can't just go around doing shit like that. I'm not a bad guy. The dog. Rex. Rescue dog. Went through shit before me."

"He's lying," the woman said.

"Shut up," the man said, spinning around to her, his composure slipping right away. And then he took another step towards Max, returning his focus. "Come on. Let's not get dramatic here. Leave me be. Walk away. It ain't your business, buddy. It ain't your fight."

And Max heard the guy. He heard him, and he hated to admit it, but he was right.

It wasn't his business.

Wasn't his fight.

He looked beyond the man at the woman on the road.

Then at the dog.

He wanted to step in.

Wanted to help them.

He gritted his teeth, looked at the man opposite, and he turned away.

"Good move," the man said.

That's when Max felt a smack over his head.

When he tumbled to the road.

Heard the dog barking.

Turned around and saw the guy standing over him.

Baseball bat in hand.

Smile on his face.

The machete on the ground and out of reach.

"Shoulda just walked away," the bloke said, lifting the baseball bat. "Shoulda just gone when you had the chance."

He went to swing the baseball bat towards Max's head.

And then Max heard a massive thump.

He lifted his hand instinctively. Expected the pain of the baseball bat to split through his already aching head.

But then he realised he hadn't felt a thing.

He opened his eyes. Looked up.

And that's when he saw him.

The man. The thug who'd dragged the woman away then attacked him.

He was bleeding from his head.

He fell, flat, on the road, right beside Max.

And right behind him, Max saw the woman. Bloodied brick in her hand.

Her eyes were wide. She looked frozen. Frozen in time. Like she couldn't actually believe what she'd just done.

She dropped the brick to the road. The dog walked up to her, staring at its owner, who grunted on the road. He wasn't dead, but he wasn't in a good way, that was for sure. Groaning. Bleeding out from a nasty crack on his head.

Max looked at the man, his head still spinning. He was lucky. Lucky to have escaped that. He would've hit him again with that baseball bat—and who knows what might've happened to him then.

He pulled himself to his feet. A little wobbly. A little dizzy.

But awake.

Awake, conscious, and alive.

He saw the woman, then. Staring wide-eyed at the fallen man, still clearly in disbelief that she'd just hit him like that.

She was young. Probably in her thirties. She looked tired. Had a few cuts and bruises, a few burn marks. Leg looked like it was bleeding.

She looked in shock.

He wanted to ask her if she was okay. If everything was fine.

But then he felt those walls erecting themselves around him again.

Like they always did.

"You should get away from here," he said. "Get out of the city. Get to the countryside. Somewhere... somewhere way out of the way. And make sure you have enough to survive on. You're going to need it. We all are."

She looked at him. And for a moment, Max wondered if she was going to ask for his help. He half expected it at this point.

He wanted to say something.

But he turned around from the woman, looked at the road he'd just run down.

It was time to go home.

He swallowed a lump in his throat.

He wanted to look back at the woman once more. To ask if she was sure she was okay.

But then he took a deep breath, and he walked.

CHAPTER TWENTY-SIX

It didn't take Seth long to realise this blackout shit was far more widespread than just the prison.

He stood on top of the bus station and took a deep breath as he looked out over the city centre. It was beautiful being up here. He used to come up here when he was a kid and just watch the world go by. Watch the buses come in and out of the station. Watch people go about their daily routines, with no idea there was somebody up there, looking down on them.

And he used to get a kick from imagining picking them up, lifting them into the sky, and squeezing them between his fingers, like ants. At pulling them out of their nice, safe lives, where they thought they were alone, where they thought they weren't being watched, and submitting them to unspoken horrors.

Why?

Out of boredom, maybe.

Out of curiosity, perhaps.

He didn't know. Why did he do anything at all, really?

He was wired up the way he was wired up. And whether people liked it or not, that's just the way he was.

He stood there in his prison gear and pictured all the fun he could be having right now. The world was clearly in the shit. He didn't know what was happening, but it didn't look good. There were fires all over the city. Smoke rising everywhere. People kicking off, fighting.

And the lights. All out. Everywhere.

He smirked. Still not quite believing his luck. Still not quite believing this wasn't some kind of dream. Because in the three years he'd been locked away, he'd had one main goal. One primary focus.

To finish what he started, what he was unable to finish, three years ago.

Because his plan was simple. His revenge plan against the police officer who wronged him. Who arrested his girlfriend, Sandy, the love of his life, taken her away from him.

Only for her to take her own life in prison.

He'd taken a lot from him. He'd killed his wife and his son. Watched them bleed.

And he'd seen the horror on the officer's face.

And then, before he could enact his final part of the revenge, the police arrived and arrested him, right away.

And at the time, Seth thought that was punishment enough. He thought that was torture enough.

But in the years since, locked inside, he'd spent the time stewing away. Thinking about what else he could do. How else he could torture that police officer for what he took from him. How he could punish him.

He never thought he'd get that opportunity.

But right now, looking down on the city as it tore itself apart, he knew he had a *perfect* opportunity.

He took a deep breath, looked over towards Fulwood, where the officer used to live, and he smiled.

He turned away from the edge of the bus station roof, and he walked away.

A ghost in the night.

CHAPTER TWENTY-SEVEN

Aoife stood over the body of the man she'd knocked to the ground—the man who'd attacked her—and she wasn't sure what to do. Wasn't sure what to think.

It was dark. Pitch black. The night had seemed endless, and yet Aoife got the weird sense that it had only just begun. So much had happened in such a short space of time. Getting the bus home. The crash. Dragging herself out of there and hearing Harry was still alive. Trying to get him out, and then the plane hitting and…

She didn't want to think about the plane crash.

About what had happened to Harry.

And what had happened to the girl.

And then she thought of the trek that followed. The sights she'd seen. The cars all piled up in the middle of the road. The fires. The looting. The chaos.

Enough signs already that everything was spiralling out of control—and this was only the first night. What happened if this lasted? If the power stayed out even longer?

Lawlessness.

Everything would be out of control.

But as she stood here, she could only think about now. About what she could do *now*.

And right now, she was standing in the middle of a street in a dodgy area over a fallen guy, a guy who she'd smacked over the head to save... whoever the man was who saved her.

She remembered the look in his eyes. That look like he was curious. Like he wanted to ask about her. Like he didn't want to be alone.

She remembered the way he'd walked away. The way he'd turned his back and wished her luck then walked before she could even ask a thing about him.

And she understood. She got it. Because she felt the same reluctance, too. A sense that she could do things on her own. That she could deal with things herself. That it was better doing things her own way and not letting anyone else be involved, ignoring any form of outside influence.

She remembered what Kayleigh said. About her being stubborn. About her thinking she knew best.

And she wondered if the reason she felt so sore about those accusations was that she had a point.

She gritted her teeth. Took a deep breath. A part of her wanted to turn around. To walk back to the flat.

But then what was at the flat?

And the guy was right. The guy who'd saved her. His words echoed what Dad told her when she was a child.

Stay out of the city, Aoife. Don't be drawn in by the material goods the city has to offer. Nature is the greatest store of all. Always.

And she'd strayed from that path through her life. She'd walked down the path of a lawyer until she quit her job. But like so many others, it was the city that drew her towards it, off nature's path. A path that she wanted to return to, now.

But right now, as she looked back towards her home, just on the outskirts of the city, she could smell smoke in the air. She was shivering and cold. And she knew the bloke was right. She needed a head start.

And yet...

The thought of being alone, as much as it had appealed to her over recent years, it scared her.

She knew about survival. But knowledge wasn't everything. Principle wasn't practice at the end of the day.

She looked back around. Over at the man, who lay in a pool of blood.

And then at the dog, Rex, beside her, wagging his little docked tail, like the pair of them were just destined to be together.

She looked up where the man who'd saved her—and who *she'd* saved—had disappeared to, and she took a deep breath.

"Come on, Rex," she said. "Let's go find that man. I think he might be worth following."

And then she walked over the fallen body of the man on the road.

* * *

Gary opened his eyes.

Saw the woman walking away.

Saw his dog, Rex, walking away with her.

His fingers twitched.

His jaw tightened.

He was going to make them pay.

CHAPTER TWENTY-EIGHT

Max kept his head down and walked.

It was dark. He didn't mind it that way. After all, it would be morning when the chaos truly took hold. When people woke up and realised the power was still out. The people who'd somehow slept through the night woke up and realised that the world had radically changed, all in a flash.

That's when things would really start to get messy. When things would really slip out of control.

He wanted to be far away from the city of Preston when that happened.

Everyone wanted to be far away from the city when that happened.

He thought of the looting that would occur. He thought of the few police officers who'd stayed on duty, trying to maintain order. He thought about the potential for military involvement and how that would rub people the wrong way. On how an attempt to create some order would have the reverse effect.

He thought about all these potential things that would happen. He thought about the fight for the final dwindling supplies in supermarkets. He thought about the lawlessness, as the bulk of the police went home to fend for themselves, no command chain to follow. He thought about the power grabs as the military attempted to control the streets, clashes growing violent and deadly. He thought about the struggles when people realised their relatives were dead already. He thought about the wounded, about the sick. He thought about the dying in hospital beds and the people who got injured and ill but wouldn't be able to seek out any care.

And viruses. Viruses would run rife. Disease would thrive in a world without sanitation.

He thought about it all, and he shuddered.

He wanted to be far away when that happened.

He walked down the street. He was still in the suburbs, but it wasn't as busy here. A few people sat outside their houses, drinking beer. A few New Year's Eve parties that had spilled out onto the lawns. And there was a weird vibe to it all. A sense that a lot of people still didn't realise quite how serious this was. That they were just going to go to bed later and hope it was all cleared up in the morning.

Max knew for a fact that wasn't going to happen.

And then he thought of the woman.

The woman he'd helped—or rather, the woman who'd helped him.

The way she'd whacked that dick over the head with a brick.

The shock on her face as she stood there, the dog by her side.

A part of him wished he'd asked her along. Because she looked lost. Lost, but tough.

But... no.

He couldn't go bringing strays along.

At the end of the day, everyone had a choice to be prepared or not. And the vast majority of the population had chosen another path.

What was his was his.

He hadn't made any mistakes.

He—

"Hey."

He heard the voice and froze.

He didn't want to turn around. Didn't want to see who might be onto him. After all, the guy from the shop he'd raided didn't look like he was the sort to give up without a fight.

And when the people from the estate he'd got into the scuffle with caught up with him... well, he didn't want to think too much about that, either.

But when Max turned around, he realised it wasn't who he expected.

It was the woman.

The woman with the dog. The woman who'd been in the fight not long ago.

She walked towards him. And there was something about her that reminded him of Kathryn, but when she was younger. Much younger.

She even sounded like her, too.

And there was something about that which made Max feel even weirder about turning her away.

But she wasn't Kathryn.

He couldn't be sentimental.

"Why are you following me?" Max asked.

The woman frowned. "Following you? How do you know I'm following you?"

"You were way behind me. Now you're here. Right where I'm heading."

"Could be a coincidence," the woman said. The dog by her side.

Max grunted. "It's like I said. You should find someplace out of the city to go. It's not safe here."

The woman sighed. "You're welcome, by the way."

"Do I owe you a thanks?"

"I saved your life."

"I think you'll find I saved your life. And doing that almost got me in deep shit. Part of why I'd rather be alone. So if you don't mind…"

Max turned and started walking.

He heard footsteps following behind.

He looked back. Glared at her.

"Firstly, that's definitely not how I remember things going down, but we'll agree to disagree on that. Secondly, it's not a crime to walk on the same road as you. Or in the same direction as you. And truth be told, I don't really have any place to go. Not really. Nowhere outside the city, anyway. You seem like you might have somewhere."

"And if you think you're joining me, you're mistaken."

The woman shrugged. "It's like I said. Nothing stopping me following you to somewhere safer."

Max sighed. He appreciated that the woman had guts. But at the same time, she was annoying.

"Look," he said. "I don't owe you a thing. But because you did bail me out before, I'll tell you what's happening here. It looks to me like an EMP has—"

"An electromagnetic pulse has triggered a blackout and wiped the power out. All forms of power. The city's going to fall into disarray in no time. And judging by the way planes fell from the sky, chances are it's a bad one. Might even be global. We have no idea of knowing. Not right away. Yeah, yeah. I know what's happening here. You don't need to EMP-splain to me."

Max gritted his teeth. Again, couldn't deny he was a little impressed. "If you know what's happening, then you'll know what you need to do."

"I know a thing or two," she said. "My dad, he… When I was younger. He taught me things. But anyway. Probably not the time for an autobiography."

"You're right about that."

"Name's Aoife, by the way."

Max nodded.

Aofie raised her eyebrows. "Well?"

"Well, what?"

"Usually when someone introduces themselves, it's the courteous thing to introduce yourself back."

"Oh," Max said. "Well, it's irrelevant anyway because you won't need to know it. But the name's Max."

"Max," Aoife said, smiling. "I would say it's a pleasure to meet you. But I'm not sure either of us shares that sentiment."

Max nodded. He kind of liked her, as much as it pained him to admit it.

"Look, Max," Aoife said. "In case you hadn't noticed, I've kind of been through a shitty few hours. I'm not going to annoy you. I'm not going to get all up in your face. I'm just going to walk the way you're walking if that's fine with you."

"And if it isn't?"

Aoife smiled. "What are you going to do about it?"

Max shook his head. Sighed. What harm was her following him doing, after all?

"You can follow," Max said. "But no talking. And especially no questions, okay? We just walk."

Aoife opened her mouth. Then she stopped. Zipped her lips with a fake zip and smiled.

Max nodded. "Good start. You're learning."

He turned around, looked towards the road out of the city, and he walked.

The woman and the dog—who she called Rex—following closely behind.

"Still not letting you off the hook for EMPsplaining, though," Aoife said.

CHAPTER TWENTY-NINE

He saw them in the distance—man, woman, and dog—and he tensed his fists.
He knew what he needed to do.

CHAPTER THIRTY

Aoife walked with Max, and she stayed true to her promise of not saying a word.

This endless night was still pitch black. No signs of sunrise approaching. She was freezing. Shivering. Probably the shock, in all truth. But she wasn't exactly going to moan about it. She didn't want to give this Max guy the satisfaction.

He seemed like an obnoxious prick, in all truth. He seemed rude and patronising, and he hadn't really shown many redeeming features, that was for sure.

But there was something about him. Something that reminded Aoife about her dad, for some reason. Something she couldn't put her finger on.

But she felt safe with him. Even though she felt ridiculous admitting that in itself.

She didn't want to be patronised.

She didn't want to feel subservient or inferior to anyone. Let alone a miserable old bloke.

She needed to look past that sense that he was a bit like her father used to be and focus on what he was *actually* like.

They were well out of the city now, but the more they walked, the more signs of disarray Aoife saw. It was the same everywhere. The cars in the middle of the road. The debris from fallen aircraft smouldering away. That constant stench of smoke hanging in the air. All the lights out, and the darkness that accompanied it.

And Aoife saw strange sights. A row of houses wiped out by a fallen helicopter. People lying dead in the street, wounded by the debris, and unable to do anything about it. Unable to find any help anywhere. The lines dead, so no way of reporting any emergency. And the ambulances unable to get anywhere anyway.

She thought of the scenes at A&E right now. And at the hospital in general. She shuddered. The thought of ICU being wiped out in an instant. Of the people desperate for medication. Old people trapped in their homes. Drunk people on New Year's Eve and the accidents they would've had, and how they'd be unable to find any sort of help.

She thought of Kayleigh and her friends, then, and forced herself not to think too much about them.

There was nothing else she could do for them. Nothing she could do for them at all. As guilty as she felt about it, she had to trust her instincts and get out of the city and into the wilderness.

Fortunately, Dad taught her a few things about survival. He didn't treat her brother the same way, but then she was always his favourite.

And besides. Her brother was an interesting character. It didn't exactly surprise her that he and Dad didn't have the best of bonds.

She looked around at Max, hoping that at this point, he might've defrosted a little bit.

"So, where are you heading?"

He glared at her.

"Oh, come on," Aoife said.

"We said no questions."

"I didn't think we *actually* meant we weren't going to exchange a word this whole bloody way."

"Well, I did."

Aoife puffed out her lips, sighed. "At least tell me a bit about yourself."

"What is there to know?"

"I dunno. I mean, I would ask if you had any family, but I figure that's unlikely the way you are."

He stopped, then. And Aoife saw his eyes widen. Just for a moment, an expression she hadn't seen from him before. Something like anger.

"Sorry," Aoife said, sensing she'd hit a sore spot. "Just making conversation."

"I'll flip it back on you then," Max said, sounding a bit pissed off.

"What about me?"

"Tell me about your life. Tell me about where you're from. And, hey. While we're at it, tell me about *your* relationships. Because it's hard to imagine you getting far in one, too, for what it's worth."

It was the most she'd heard him speak, and his words stung a little. And they further reinforced Aoife's opinion that he wasn't all that great a guy.

But then she sensed there was pain beneath those words.

But what he'd said about her. About it being hard to imagine her having a personal life of her own, too…

"What do you mean by that?"

Max turned around, shook his head. "We said no talking."

"I want to know what you meant when you said—"

"I didn't mean anything," Max said. "I just… Don't go asking people about themselves. Don't go making assumptions. Especially if you aren't willing to talk about them yourself."

Aoife heard Max's words, and she wanted to argue. But she figured he might have a point.

Did she really want to go telling him about Jason?

About what happened with him?

About what he'd *chosen* over her?

Maybe Max was right. Maybe it was better to stay quiet.

She walked along, Rex wandering beside her, happy and oblivious to everything going on. And no matter what happened, at least she had his company. All she needed when it came down to it.

"Shit," Max said.

She looked up. "What?"

Max was walking over to something lying on the side of the road.

It was a motorbike.

An old bike. Silver. Looked like a classic type, although Aoife couldn't pretend to know much about bikes.

The biker lying dead by its side.

The keys still inserted.

Max lifted it up. "An old Yamaha. Old enough not to be computerised, too. If we're in luck…"

He started up the bike, and it came to life.

He smiled for the first time Aoife had ever seen. Chuckled a little.

And it felt weird, seeing the absurdity of a dead man's bike being stolen, and yet it being treated as such a normality.

It felt *wrong*.

"A working bike," he said. "Not an opportunity anyone wants to pass up."

He looked at Aoife, and Aoife sensed there was a question, there. Sensed that he wanted to ask her if she wanted to join him. Like it was unspoken. Was he waiting for her to ask? To make the first move?

Dammit. She didn't want to give him that satisfaction.

"Well," he said. "It's… I guess it's going to be hard carrying a dog on the bike. Especially a big dog like that."

Aoife's stomach sank. "So you're leaving us?"

"I thought... Well. I thought you said you were just going the same way as me?"

Aoife wanted to tell Max that as much as she didn't like him and as much as he seemed a bit of a pig, she kind of liked him.

She sensed something there, under the surface.

Hidden pain.

She wanted to ask him if he'd stay with her, if she could join him.

She wanted to at least ask him where he was going.

But she couldn't.

She just couldn't.

She went to open her mouth to say something when she heard footsteps behind.

"Hey, bitch," a voice said.

Aoife spun around, jumping out of her skin.

Beside her, Rex growled.

And when Aoife saw who was standing there, she could barely believe it.

She thought she was staring at a ghost.

But it was him.

Burned. Wounded. Covered in blood.

But it was him.

"Harry?" she said.

CHAPTER THIRTY-ONE

Aoife stared at Harry standing there and couldn't quite believe what she was looking at.

He was alive. More battered and bruised than she remembered, but there was no mistaking it was him.

It was Harry.

The last time she'd seen him, he'd been shouting for help, trapped inside the same bus she only narrowly managed to escape from.

She'd raced away from that bus in search of someone who could help, but then out of nowhere, a plane hurtled from the sky. Sent the whole bus up in flames.

And now he was here. Dried blood all over his face. His dark hair dripping sweat.

And a look in his bloodshot eyes of hatred.

"Harry?" she said. "How... how did you..."

"What?" he said. "Surprised to see me?"

"I—I—"

"Lost for words? Yeah. I would be too. If I'd left someone for dead, I'd be exactly the same."

He walked towards Aoife, and she heard Rex growling beside her. A protective growl. Kicking his back legs a little. Docked tail definitely not wagging now.

"You left me for dead," he said. "You could've helped me. But you didn't. Because of some shitty argument we had before the crash."

"That's not true," Aoife said.

"Bullshit," Harry shouted. And then she saw in the moonlight the scratches across his face. The scratches she realised she'd given him. "You turned your back on me, and you ran away from me. I barely got out. I barely escaped. But I did. I did, and now I'm here. No fucking thanks to you."

Aoife stared at Harry, and she shook her head. She felt so guilty for leaving him behind, for leaving him to die.

But he was here now.

He'd managed to escape.

He'd managed to fight his way free of the bus.

And for some reason, she couldn't shake the feeling deep within that maybe things would have been easier if he hadn't shown up out of the blue.

Because he was alive, and he clearly wanted some sort of revenge, which was a problem.

He stepped towards Aoife. Rex growled even more. Max was deadly quiet behind them all.

"I didn't want you to die," Aoife said.

"Bullshit. At least on the bus when you were scratching my face like a fucking animal, you were honest."

"Harry," Aoife said, digging her heels in. "I wanted to help. I had to save myself. I tried to find help. I tried. You can believe me or not. But that's how it went down."

But he kept on walking towards her.

Walking with anger on his face.

Like he wanted to hurt her.

He stepped up to her as Rex started to bark at him.

"Can you shut your dog up? It's getting on my—agh!"

Rex bit his ankle.

Harry fell to the floor, screaming like a child.

And as Aoife stood there, watching him roll about so pitifully, she kind of wanted to leave Rex to it. Because as much as she hadn't wanted him to die, Harry was quite clearly a piece of shit. He'd spat in her face. And way before that, he'd made it clear he was misogynistic trash.

But then, on the other hand… well. He'd been through a lot of shit tonight too. A lot of trauma. He was bound to be fired up right now.

"Rex, stop," Aoife said.

Right on cue, Rex backed off, stepped away.

She stood over Harry, then. Looked down at him as he clutched his ankle, rolling around on the ground.

"Listen to me," she said. "I'm not here to have some futile little petty argument about whether I did or didn't walk away. On whether I did or didn't leave you to die. It's bullshit. All I'm here for is to get out of the city. I don't want to be held up by dickheads like you. So you've got a choice, here. You can get up, and you can actually stop whinging and acting like an adult. Or you can stay there, and you can get fucked, quite frankly."

Harry looked up at her. The attention he was giving his ankle seemed to have faded now.

"You're crazy," he said.

"Maybe so," Aoife said. "But that's how it is."

She held out a hand.

He looked at it, just for a second.

And then he ignored it and clambered to his feet.

"Wait," Max said. The first things he'd said in this entire exchange. "I remember you."

Harry looked over at him. And Max looked back at him, smirk on his face.

"The dick trying to get in the nightclub I was working at. Surprised you made it this far."

Harry shook his head. "Oh, piss off."

"Strongly considering it," Max said, perched on that motorcycle. "*Strongly* considering it."

Aoife looked at Harry, and she didn't know what to say to him. Didn't know what to suggest. He'd clearly followed her here. He clearly just wanted to confront her.

But right now, she had bigger priorities on her mind.

"I don't know what your plan is," she said. "But I'm getting out of the city."

"I might just join you," Harry said.

"You're not welcome."

"I can walk with you if I want to walk with you. No rules against that. Right?"

She opened her mouth to argue, then she remembered saying the same thing to Max and sensed her hypocrisy.

She closed her mouth. Sighed. "You can walk the way I'm going if you want to. But believe me. You aren't coming with me."

"You owe me that much."

"No," Aoife said. "I owe you literally nothing."

She went to turn around when she heard something up ahead.

Something from the direction of the houses.

A group of people, running their way.

"Give Rex back!" one of them shouted. Blood trickling down his face.

The bloke she'd attacked.

And he wasn't alone.

He was with four other people, all with baseball bats, all running towards them.

She swallowed a lump in her throat. "What do we do..."

And then she stopped.

Because she heard an engine rev up.

She turned around, and she saw Max turning the bike.

"Max?" she said. "What..."

"Sorry," he said. "Nothing personal. But this isn't my business. Good luck."

He turned around, and he drove off into the distance.

And the group of thugs got closer and closer.

CHAPTER THIRTY-TWO

"Well," Harry said. "It looks like you're in deep shit now."

Aoife watched Max disappear into the distance on the motorbike he'd found. He didn't look back. And she felt betrayed. She hated that she felt this way. She hated feeling so dependent on somebody, especially somebody she didn't even know, not really.

But then there'd been something about him. Something that, dare she say it, reminded her of her dad.

She gritted her teeth. Shook her head. He didn't owe her anything. She'd walked with him for a while, but they were just strangers at the end of the day.

Nobody owed anybody anything.

She heard the group running towards her, towards Harry, and felt a knot of fear in her stomach.

"I mean," Harry said. "They don't sound like they're best pleased with you."

"Shut up."

"You have a real way of making friends, don't you?"

"I said shut up, okay?"

Harry raised his hands, which were cut and bloodied. "I'm just saying. It looks like someone's finally gonna make you pay for your actions. The past always catches up with you in the end."

Aoife looked around at the approaching group, and she hated to admit it, but she was afraid. She didn't like feeling afraid. Didn't like that sense of fear. It was the sense of vulnerability that bothered her, more than most things in life. The sense that someone might have the satisfaction of feeling stronger than her, somehow.

She saw them approaching, and as much as she wanted to stand her ground, as much as she wanted to show her strength and stand up to them, she knew she had to run.

She turned and ran as quickly as her sore leg would allow.

She ran in the direction of Max's bike, and she heard Harry shouting for her.

"Hey! I can't run too well here. Don't fucking leave me again."

And when she looked back at him, she felt bad for him, once again.

Because looking at it from his perspective, much of a shit as he was, for just a moment...

She'd left him in that bus to fend for himself.

And then, when he'd approached her about it, her dog had attacked him.

She looked at him and the approaching group.

And she saw Rex standing his ground and barking, too.

She knew she should take a leaf out of Max's book. She knew she should just drop her petty attachments and run like the fucking wind.

But that wasn't her.

She took a deep breath, gritted her teeth, and walked back.

When she got back to Harry's side, she regretted it right away.

The man she'd hit over the head stood right there, right opposite her. Blood trickled all down his face. He didn't look good.

"Take my dog?" he said, baseball bat in hand. "Hit me over the head? You're a real piece of work; you know that?"

"Come on," Aoife said, knowing she should hold her tongue but unable to—a problem she'd always had. "You were barely looking after the dog in the first place. One less mouth to feed if you let me take him anyway."

"She's a right bitch, Gary," a bloke by his side said. "You should teach her a lesson, lad."

"Yeah," Aoife said, heart racing, adrenaline surging. "Fighting amongst ourselves. That's really going to achieve a hell of a lot right now, isn't it?"

The man called Gary stepped forward. Walked right up to Aoife, right up in her face. She could smell his sour breath. Stunk of booze. And his eyes were massive like he'd taken drugs.

He looked dangerous. And she couldn't help feeling a little afraid of him.

But she'd be damned if she didn't stand up to someone when she felt like they were wronging her.

"I should fucking kick the shit out of you," Gary said. And then he checked her out. "But maybe we can all have some more fun with you."

He scanned her from head to toe.

Licked his lips.

She tensed her jaw, gritted her teeth, and got ready to fight with everything she had.

But she couldn't shake her fear.

Couldn't shake her horror.

Couldn't—

"Leave her alone."

She wasn't sure where the voice came from. Not at first.

But then, as Gary looked around, she saw exactly where he was looking, too.

"Who the fuck are you?" Gary asked.

Harry stood tall. Covered in blood. Shaking.

But standing his ground.

And standing up for Aoife.

Gary walked towards him. Gary's friends walked towards him. All of them turning their attention towards Harry now. Circling him.

"I asked you a question," Gary said. "Who the fuck are you?"

"It doesn't matter who I am," Harry said. "Leave her alone. Move on. Surely you've got something better to do right now."

There was silence. A few laughs from the group.

A smile across Gary's face, even though he was quite clearly pissed off, too.

"Wow," Gary said. "Confident. I like that."

He looked around at Aoife, and a grin stretched across his face.

"This your boyfriend?" he asked.

"No. He's—"

"What the hell. I don't give a shit."

And then he turned on Harry.

Whacked him over the side of the head with his baseball bat.

And then his friends descended on him as he fell to the floor and started beating him to a pulp.

CHAPTER THIRTY-THREE

Max accelerated forward and didn't look back.

It was still dark, but he could see the sky turning bluer now as morning approached. He definitely wanted to be far away from the city when the sun rose. People were going to lose their shit when they woke up, hungover, and in realisation that the power was still out and that there was no information at all about what the hell was going on.

Max gritted his teeth and focused on the road ahead. He couldn't go as fast as he wanted because there were so many obstacles on the street. Debris. Cars. But he was going quick enough. As quick as he needed to go.

He'd be home soon, and he could focus on the next step.

He knew there were more things he could do with stocking up on. Supplies for his bug-out bag.

But he wasn't taking any chances anymore.

He moved the bike around the side of a fallen telegraph pole when he swore he heard a shout behind.

He looked back, and he felt a bit of guilt. Because he'd left Aoife and the dog, Rex, all on their own back there. He didn't give a shit about the lad, Harry. He seemed like a right arsehole, and he wasn't going to feign sympathy for him.

But he did feel a bit bad about Aoife.

He turned around. He shouldn't feel bad, and he knew it. She wasn't his responsibility. They were strangers. They'd just run into each other. He'd helped her out, and she'd helped him out.

But at the end of the day, they weren't bound together. They were individuals.

And Max had made himself pretty clear. He was going back home, and Aoife could find her own way.

He didn't owe her anything. He was his own man, and he shouldn't go feeling responsible for anyone else.

But still, he couldn't shake the feeling that he'd done something bad. That he'd abandoned Aoife.

He grunted. She was tough. She'd make it. If she had any sense about her, she'd turn around and abandon that Harry prick *and* the dog. They were millstones around her neck. They'd hold her back.

He wondered whether he really believed that she was going to be okay back there or if he was just trying to convince himself.

He looked at the road ahead, illuminated by the bike's lights, which seemed weird amidst this landscape of darkness. He needed to keep going. Needed to crack on. Couldn't get caught up in fears about what he was leaving behind. Couldn't get caught up in any kind of attachment.

He looked ahead, saw a taxi in the road in front of him. Slowed down, worked his way around it.

He glanced to the side, and he stopped.

Sitting in the back of the taxi, he saw a boy.

He was young. Sixteen or seventeen, he'd guess.

He recognised him.

He had a large metal pole right through his chest.

Blood trickling down his face.

His eyes wide, his glasses smashed.

It was the boy he'd let in the nightclub.

The boy who'd staggered out and Max helped into a taxi.

He was dead.

It looked like some scaffolding had come through the windscreen, piercing both the driver and the boy in the back.

And as Max stared at him, he felt this sense of responsibility again.

This sense that he'd done this.

That the whole reason the kid was here in the first place was because he'd put him in here.

He gritted his teeth. Shook his head.

But he couldn't shake the images flashing in his mind now.

David.

Going into his son's bedroom.

Seeing him there.

Seeing the blood.

And...

"No," he said.

He biked on. But he wasn't focused. He was distracted. Lost. He kept on bumping into cars. Tumbling over debris.

And all that time, he kept on getting new flashes in his mind.

Of Aoife.

Screaming.

Of those thugs whacking her over the head with baseball bats.

Of her bloodied corpse.

He squeezed his eyes shut and stopped.

Sat there on the bike, heart pounding.

And then he looked back, a bitter taste in his mouth.

He didn't know what to do for the best.

Didn't know where to go.

But he lowered his head, and he sighed.

He put his foot down, trying to get the image of the boy with the scaffolding through his chest out of his mind.

The images of Aoife out of his mind.

Of David out of his mind.
And he drove.

CHAPTER THIRTY-FOUR

Aoife watched Gary and his friends bury their boots and their baseball bats into Harry's curled-up body, and she wished she could do more.

The scene was brutal. More horrifying than anything she'd ever witnessed. They were on him like a pack of animals. Kicking him. Punching him. Whacking him with whatever they were holding. Baseball bats, cricket bats, all kinds of things.

And she could see Harry in the middle of them all. Covering his face with his broken fingers. The blood all over him, even more now than there was before—and there already was a lot before.

And the gasps he let out. The whimpers and winces.

The sound of a baseball bat cracking against his skull.

"Stop it!" Aoife shouted.

She was paralysed. Paralysed with fear. Because Harry didn't deserve this. Nobody deserved this. He'd stood up for her. Despite everything, he'd actually stood up for her, and this was what he got for it.

She couldn't just stand here.

She had to do something.

She had to help.

"Stop," she said, racing forward. "Stop this. Now!"

And then she felt a crack across her face.

Went tumbling back and hit the road, thumping her head in the process.

She lay there, ears ringing, the taste of blood filling up in her mouth. And as she lay there, Rex barking by her side, she felt helpless. Totally helpless. She'd always prided herself on being strong. On being able to stand up for herself.

And she'd got even tougher over the last few years, especially after what she went through with Jason.

She thought of entering that hotel room.

Of seeing him...

No.

She didn't want to think about that. Not now.

She sat there on the road and watched as the men returned their attention to Harry. And she wanted to help him. She didn't want to abandon him. Not again.

She forced herself to her feet and tensed her fists.

She launched herself at one of the men, who she recognised as Gary, scratching his face.

He elbowed her.

Knocked her back again.

"Bitch," he spat.

He turned to her. Walked over to her. Held his baseball bat in hand. Beside, Rex barked and growled at him.

"You're with her now, you stupid fucking mutt. Which means you're fair game."

He pulled back the baseball bat.

Went to swing it at Rex.

"No!" Aoife shouted.

And then it all happened so fast.

The sound of an engine.

Revving up, right by her.

And then a bolt of light flying past her.

Slamming into Gary.

Sending him hurtling back.

And then driving through his friends, making them jump out of the way.

It took Aoife a few moments to realise what was happening here.

But then she saw it.

Max.

Max was back.

He lifted a machete. Pulled it back and turned on the gang.

"You get the hell away from him. And you stay the hell away from him. Okay? Because if you don't, you're fucked. My friends are heading down here, and they'll back me up. So leave him alone, leave her alone, and leave the dog alone. Understand?"

Aoife's heart raced as she saw him standing there, right before the bike. Her overwhelming emotion was a sense of relief. He'd come back for her. He'd actually come back for her.

"Aoife," he said. "On the bike. Now."

Aoife narrowed her eyes. She looked at Harry, whose eyes were swollen over, and who'd been beaten to a pulp.

And then at Rex. Barking away.

"But... but we can't leave them."

"If you want to get out of here, get on the bike. Now."

She opened her mouth to argue. But she knew she didn't have any argument.

Harry was as good as dead.

There was nothing she could do for him.

And as much as she wanted to protect Rex... he wasn't her dog. Right?

Two of the men stood there, baseball bats still in hand. Gary lay in front of the bike, bleeding badly. She dreaded to think what sort of damage Max had done and couldn't quite believe what she'd witnessed.

"On the bike, Aoife. Now!"

She looked at Harry. And then she looked at Rex. And she wanted to apologise to them. She wanted to say sorry for walking away. That she had no other choice. This was her only option.

She gritted her teeth. Tensed her fists.

Started walking.

And then...

"No," she said.

Max frowned. "What?"

"I'm not leaving Harry here. I'm not leaving Rex here. You... you go if you have to. You do whatever you have to do. But I'm not leaving them behind."

Max narrowed his eyes. The two men still standing looked from her to Max, like they were reading the room here.

"Aoife," he said. "Stop playing around. If you want to get out of this, you need to come with me. Now."

She took a deep breath, and she shook her head. "You might find it easy to walk away. But I don't. I'm not leaving them. I'm not leaving anyone else. Not again."

Max opened his mouth. Then he closed it. Clearly pissed off at Aoife.

"Then you've made your choice," he said.

He turned around to walk back to the bike.

That's when one of the men rushed over to him, lifted their bat.

"Nice bike," he said.

Swung the baseball bat over Max's head.

Knocked him to the road.

"Don't mind if we take it," he said.

He jumped on to it. And the other guy jumped on the back, too. With Max's bag and his machete, too.

And then, they drove.

CHAPTER THIRTY-FIVE

Max opened his eyes and immediately felt a sense of dread surge through him.

It was light. Far lighter than when his eyes had closed. Not exactly morning light, but definitely getting that way. Dawn approaching. A cold chill to the air, which went without saying in the middle of winter.

A sore head. Really damned sore. He wasn't sure why, only that something had gone down. Something had gone down, and...

Shit.

The gang.

The gang of thugs who'd stolen his bike.

One of them must've hit him over the head, and...

"Awake?" a voice said.

He turned around and saw Aoife standing beside him.

He felt a combination of emotions at seeing her. Part of him felt relieved. Relieved that she was alive. Relieved that she was okay.

And relieved that she was still here.

There was a weird look on her face, in her wide eyes. A combination of emotions, clearly.

"I stayed here with you. In case you were wondering."

Max lifted himself up. Saw Rex by Aoife's side, growling away. He looked around. He could see a body right by him. The body of the bloke, Gary. The one he'd rode the bike right into, splitting his chest on the wheels. "The others?"

"Long gone," Aoife said.

"How long have I been out?"

"Not long. Half an hour. Something like that. But don't get any ideas above your station. I'm only still here 'cause of Harry."

Max narrowed his eyes. He wasn't sure what she meant at first.

Not until he looked around and saw that lad, Harry, lying there in a bloodied heap beside him.

His face was badly bruised. His eyelids were all swollen over and purple. He was breathing heavily and strained. And as much as Max didn't like the guy, he felt this instant sadness. Because he didn't deserve that shit. He looked in pain. Nobody deserved pain like that. Especially not at the hands of a bunch of thugs the likes of which they'd just run into.

"He—he doesn't look good," Max said, standing up, walking over to him. "I'm not sure he's—"

And then he felt a slap, right across his face, which was already sore. A slap out of nowhere.

Aoife's eyes were wide. She looked pissed. "You could've stayed."

"I came back for you. Lost my bloody bike in the process."

"You could've stayed," she repeated. "You drove off. You... you left us. And then this happened. You didn't have to walk away. You didn't have to leave us."

She turned around, then. Walked over to Harry's side. Her entire demeanour shifted as if she were suddenly not proud of herself for showing how emotional she was.

Max stood there, and he felt bad. He felt awkward. Because she was right. He didn't need to drive away. He regretted it the moment he did it.

And he regretted it even more when he saw the kid in the taxi.

"I came back because I didn't want to leave you here on your own," Max said.

"Well congratulations for that. I hope you feel good about yourself."

Max gritted his teeth and sighed. He wanted to open up to Aoife. He wanted to apologise. He wanted to tell her about Kathryn, and David, and everything that happened.

He wanted to tell her the truth.

He wasn't sure why he was so compelled to tell her the truth... but he was.

But then he took a deep breath. Swallowed a lump in his throat.

He didn't know what to do next, only that Harry was in a bad way.

"Let me see to him," Max said.

"I'm sure you'll be an expert at bedside manner."

"I was a medic in the army for a while," Max said. "I know a thing or two. Bit rusty but might be able to help."

He walked over to Harry, and he felt a knot in his chest. The kid was in a bad way. Really bad way. Swollen eyes. Grunting. Choking on his own blood. Barely even seemed conscious.

"I wish there were more we could do for him," Max said. "But without ambulances, without any way of properly treating him..."

"We have to try," Aoife said.

Max heard her words, and they echoed his own pain. His pain about losing Kathryn and David. His pain about not trying harder so many times.

And the pain of still losing when he *had* tried.

"I'm just not sure what we—"

"There's a medical centre not far from here," Aoife said.

"It won't be safe."

"I don't care. We—we need to help him. He... he stood up for me. He stood up for me. He can't die now. Not... We have to help him, Max. Please."

He heard Aoife's voice, and as much as he knew it wasn't practical, as much as he knew it was a batshit crazy idea, he sighed and nodded. "I'll put something together."

He walked away. Walked off down the street in search of something they could use, fully aware that this was a waste of time.

But what if it wasn't?

What if there was a chance?

He found a surfboard atop a car just a bit further down. Dragged it off there. And then he found some old rope in the back of an abandoned jeep and tied it around it.

They could pull Harry along. It would take time, and it would slow them down, but it was something.

He rushed back to Aoife, feeling a strange sense of achievement.

And when he got there, he saw her crying, leaning right by his side.

He knew what she was crying about right away.

She turned around. Tears in her eyes, tears she was quite clearly trying to hide.

And she shook her head.

"He's gone," she said. "It's too late. He's—he's gone."

CHAPTER THIRTY-SIX

Max and Aoife walked out of the suburbs and through the surrounding countryside, not saying much at all. The sun was rising. Looked beautiful. Max always enjoyed a good sunrise. It cast an orange glow over the fields. The suburban neighbourhood they were in was quiet. Surreal, really. There was a motorway bridge over the top of the suburbs, and it was usually pretty busy and noisy at this time. But right now, it was silent. Cars were piled up there. Some of them had crashed into one another.

It was weird seeing it so busy and yet so silent. Like looking at a film set.

Aoife walked by Max's side, Rex between them. They hadn't said much at all on the journey so far. In all truth, they hadn't even said where they were going. Max was quite obviously heading back home to his cottage in the middle of nowhere on the outskirts of Beacon Fell. Aoife seemed to be walking with him.

And after the incident with Harry, the guilt she seemed to be feeling, he wasn't exactly going to turn her away right now.

Especially because he was feeling pretty guilty about the whole thing too.

He was going to get home. And she could stay, for a bit.

But forget that. He could worry about that later.

He felt like he owed her. As much as he didn't owe a soul.

He thought about the people he'd let down. The people he could've saved. The people he'd turned away from.

And as much as he didn't know Aoife, as much as he didn't have a connection to her... he wasn't going to turn his back on her.

"You okay?" he asked.

She turned around, glared at him. "What do you think?"

"I'm just asking. What happened back there... it was rough."

"Like you care," Aoife said, looking away.

Max gritted his teeth. "I do care."

"Funny way of showing it."

"Look," Max said. "I came back for you. But anyway. Forget it. Better to focus on the road. Better to keep walking."

He looked around at these suburban houses. And he felt sadness. The sun had risen. Which meant soon they'd find out the power still wasn't back on. That the police or anybody hadn't been out to help.

And panic would set in. Fast.

The looting would start in earnest today.

The rush for supplies would get messy, very, very quickly.

Max felt far better off for being away from the city centre, that was for sure.

"I left him," Aoife said.

Max sighed. "What?"

"I left him. And I could've... I could've helped him. None of this had to happen."

Max sighed. "I'm sorry. I know how tough it is."

"What do you know?" Aoife said dismissively.

"More than you realise," Max shouted.

He regretted it, right away. Turned around. But he wished he'd never said anything. Wished he'd never brought any attention to himself in that way.

Because he could see the look in Aoife's eyes.

Inquisitiveness.

Curiosity.

"What happened to you?" she asked.

"It doesn't matter."

"Something happened to you. To make you so cold. What was it?"

He heard the ringing in his ears.

Saw the memory in his head.

He saw the whole scene dancing before his eyes again.

And as much as he didn't want to tell Aoife the truth about his past, about everything, he couldn't hold off any longer.

"Three years ago," he said, the words spilling out and lifting a weight from his shoulders in an instant, "I was a police officer. I decided to take an extra week of day shifts to cover for a colleague. My wife, Kathryn. She wasn't happy. Because we'd planned on going away to the Lakes for the weekend with our son. David.

"It was the Wednesday night. I remember it well. Not hearing from Kathryn, which was weird because we always text during the day. Getting back late. Stepping inside and seeing all the lights were off. Then finding her there. Blood all over the place. Stabbed."

Aoife didn't say a word.

She just looked on, pale as a ghost.

"I rushed over to her side," Max said. "I wanted to know she was okay. I wanted to believe that because I was there, I could help her. Save her. But she'd been there for a while. Bleeding out. Kept a prisoner in her own home. And she was saying something to me. Not asking for help or anything like that but asking me to check on David. Our son."

Aoife stared with wide eyes at Max.

"I rushed into his bedroom, and I..."

He shook his head.

"I was too late," he said. "The man who killed him... He was there. Smiling. Gloating. Some revenge or other for arresting his girlfriend. The police got there before I could kill him. Before I could do anything to him. And in a way... in a way, that made it worse. Not being able to punish him for what he did, there and then. But we shouldn't have even been home. We should've gone. And that was on me."

He looked up at Aoife, a weight rising from his shoulders at even speaking about it.

He turned around and went on walking.

"So I do understand," Max said. "More than you'd ever believe."

He walked. Walked on in silence. And he expected Aoife to say something to him. Something judgemental. Like he deserved it.

But she was silent.

Really silent.

And then, as if sensing she'd been quiet for too long, she spoke.

"I'm sorry for what you went through," she said. "I can't... I can't imagine the pain you must've felt. But I... I know what it's like to lose someone. I know what it's like to feel like you have the power to save someone but can't do anything in the end. I know it's different, but... but my boyfriend. My ex. Jason. He... I thought we had a perfect relationship. Engaged. So sweet. Got married. And then... and then I found him on the honeymoon. Masturbating. I wondered what he was looking at, at first. I was a bit pissed. But then I saw the page had frozen and... They were children. There was no getting away from it. They were kids."

Max grunted. "Shit."

"We broke up immediately. But despite everything... I still felt like I wanted to help him. Like I wanted to believe this was just a character flaw. A shard of glass that could be removed. And that he could be fixed. We... we agreed he was going to go to the police with me. But it didn't happen like that. He took his own life before he could have the chance. And I was too late to save him. Because I was with another guy."

Max looked back at Aoife. He heard the pain in her voice. And it reflected his pain. The pain he felt.

"I'm sorry you went through that," he said.

She looked up at him. Nodded.

"The person who... who did this to you. To your family. What was he called?"

Max narrowed his eyes.

Thought of Seth.

"It doesn't matter," he said.

Aoife opened her mouth. She had that haunted expression to her face again.

And then she closed her mouth. "It... it doesn't matter."

Max nodded. "Right."

It felt like there was more to be said.

It felt like a bond had opened between them.

A connection.

And that felt dangerous.

She went to smile at Max when he turned around.

Walked on.

It was time to get back home.

But he couldn't deny he liked Aoife.

CHAPTER THIRTY-SEVEN

Seth stood outside the house it all unfolded at three long years ago, and he smiled.

It was morning now. The sun had just risen. And it was truly beautiful. Walking in the world a free man, he'd almost forgotten what it felt like. The sound of birdsong. The smell of the morning frost. The feel of the icy grass crunching beneath his footsteps. He could get used to being a free man, that was for sure.

But he wasn't here to be sentimental.

He was here to finish a job he wanted to finish three years ago.

The house he was at was just as he remembered. Semi-detached. Nice neighbourhood. And seeing it looking so similar to how it used to look gave him hope. Because maybe he still lived here. The detective, Max. The man who ruined his life. Who took everything away from him.

The man who he still wanted revenge against, for all he'd taken from him.

Arresting him. Picking on him, time and time again. That was understandable. Forgivable, even.

But for taking Sandy away from him.

For getting her arrested.

And for her to take her life in prison...

That he couldn't forgive.

Because Sandy was everything to him.

He walked up to the door of the house. It looked like the power was still out everywhere. The cars on the road. The people standing outside their houses, chatting to their neighbours. And in the silence, a real palpable sense that things were on the brink. On the precipice. On the verge of falling apart.

And times of chaos were Seth's favourite time to operate.

Chaos was the best cover.

He stopped at the front door. Held up a shaking hand. He wondered how he was going to go about this. Part of him just wanted to look the officer, Max, in the eye and smile. He wanted to look at him like he'd won. Like he was victorious. Like he was still here, and he was still haunting him.

And then force Max into doing something he really regretted.

The other part of him wanted to go inside his home, take whatever life he'd rebuilt for himself away from him, and finish his life, once and for all.

Just as he wanted to do three years ago, when the police showed up out of nowhere and ended Seth's revenge prematurely, right in its tracks.

He knocked on the door, gritted his teeth, and he waited.

At first, nothing. And that filled him with concern, for a moment. Because what if the house was empty? What if there was nobody here? Where would he go from here? What else did he have?

He was about to knock again when he saw a figure approaching the door.

He gritted his teeth.

Held his breath.

And then the door opened.

The bad news?

It wasn't Max.

It was a woman.

Holding a baby in her arms.

She looked young. Probably too young to be Max's wife. Which pissed Seth off slightly. But there could still be hope, right?

She glared at him. "Yes?"

"Sorry," Seth said, remembering his best manners. "I was just... Does Max still live here?"

"Max?" the woman said. "No. He... Who are you? It's—it's really early."

"Sorry," Seth said. "I just... I was driving through, and my car broke down. I had an old friend who lived here. Thought he could put me up for a little while. Until the power comes back. Anyway. Sorry to bother you."

Seth turned around, seething. He was half-tempted to attack the woman just for not being who he wanted to come to the door.

"Hold on," she said.

Seth turned around. "Yeah?"

"Max, you said? The guy who used to own this place? I think I've got his new address somewhere. If you can bear with me a minute."

Seth's eyes lit up. He went from hating this woman to loving her in the space of a moment. "Only if that's no trouble to you."

"Sure," she said. "Just... just give me a sec. It's around here somewhere. You can... you can..."

And then she stopped.

And Seth knew why. He could see it in her eyes. That uncertainty. That hesitation. That sense that there was something just *off* about him, that he'd seen in the eyes of so many already.

She was going to ask him inside.

And then she'd stopped herself.

She smiled at him, out of politeness. "I'll be with you in a sec."

"Sure," Seth said.

He watched her turn around. Watched her walk into that house.

And Seth walked in after her.

He stood there in the hallway.

Smelled the sweet flowers in the air.

The air freshener, bitter.

He looked over at the kitchen door. Saw the spot he'd stabbed her in the stomach, his sweet life.

And then the room beside.

The little boy's room.

He smiled.

"Sorry," the woman said, making him jump a little.

"Oh," Seth said. "Sorry. Excuse my nosiness. I shouldn't have come in here."

She looked at him, a bit uncertain, piece of paper in hand.

Then she handed it over.

"This... this is where he moved to. I hope it's helpful."

Seth looked down at the address.

Looked back at the woman and smiled.

"Thank you. Really."

He turned around to the front door.

He knew he should just walk away. Just go, without saying anything else.

And then he stopped because he couldn't help himself.

"Someone died here, you know?"

He looked around at her.

Saw the way her eyes stared at him.

That baby boy crying in her arms.

"Anyway," Seth said, cutting through the tension in the air. "Thank you for the address. You've helped me more than you'll ever know."

And before the woman could say another word, he stepped outside the door, out into the world again.

He looked down at the note in his hand.

Smiled.

He knew exactly where he needed to go.

CHAPTER THIRTY-EIGHT

Max couldn't describe the relief he felt when he saw his house right up ahead.

It was morning, and it was bright. Sunny. And even though it was slap bang in the middle of winter, he actually felt pretty warm. He knew it was probably just the fact he'd been walking all night. But this was the first day of a new year. And in a way, the first day of a new way of life.

And as terrifying as that notion was... he'd made this place home. And that gave him some source of optimism.

Because the whole part of the journey he was scared about most was getting out of the city. Especially on New Year's Eve. Getting out of the city and getting back home.

And sure. It wasn't perfect here. He had things stocked up here. Things that would help him survive. He had supplies. And he had skills.

But it wouldn't be enough. He'd have to take trips out. Supply runs. If this blackout really was as bad as it seemed—and he had no reason to believe it wasn't pretty damned serious—then he was in a good position. He had a head start.

But things were going to get very nasty in the cities very fast. And he was glad to be far, far away from it all.

"This your home?"

Max heard Aoife's voice, and he looked around. It'd been a tiring night, and it showed on Aoife's face. She looked pale. Seriously worn out.

But then he supposed he wouldn't look too pretty, either. It'd been an exhausting ordeal. The pain. The loss.

And as Max looked at Aoife, as he looked at the dog, Rex, he never thought he'd find himself admitting this, but he actually kind of liked her company.

He hadn't thought about the future yet. He hadn't thought about the next step. He was pretty set on being alone. After all, that was the best way. Not just for him, but for everyone.

But seeing Aoife standing here, seeing Rex between them... he couldn't deny that there was something about their company he enjoyed.

And that scared him. Because this wasn't the way it was supposed to go. This wasn't the way he was supposed to live his life. He was supposed to be on his own now. He wasn't supposed to make connections. He wasn't supposed to *like* people.

And he wasn't even sure what it was about Aoife he liked. She definitely seemed a bit stuck up. A bit rude. And he'd probably ended up in the shit more because of her, because of the battles she'd got herself caught up in.

Was it that there was something about her that reminded him of Kathryn?

A younger Kathryn?

He swallowed a lump in his throat. He couldn't think of Kathryn. Thinking of Kathryn just brought pain. And it took him down a road he didn't want to go down.

"This is my place," Max said.

Aoife smiled. "Seems nice. Perfect for someone like you."

"Someone like me?"

"Someone who isn't exactly going to be hosting barbecues for the neighbours."

"Hey," Max said, walking slowly towards his detached house now. Trees all around. The house itself, a little worn, a little tired. Needed a bit of work doing. Work he had no real motivation to do. "I used to host a mean barbecue back in the day."

"Oh yeah?"

"Oh yeah. Could start a barbecue out of nothing. That's the problem. People think they need all this fancy as fuck equipment to get one going. But it's nature's gift. Fire."

"Well, if the power stays out long enough, you might find yourself hosting a few more barbecues."

"Nah," Max said. "My hosting days are over."

"Me and Rex might want to join you, though. And hey. I'm decent at hunting, from what I can remember from being a kid, anyway. Stuff my dad taught me."

Max felt caught. Caught at a crossroads. He thought the girl might be hinting. Hinting at wanting to stay.

But then there was this roadblock. This roadblock he'd erected himself. A roadblock that stopped him wanting to let anyone else in.

"Don't you have a family to get back to or anything?"

Aoife smiled. "My dad died a few years back. I never knew my mum. I grew up with my auntie for the bulk of my childhood. And my brother... well. We never really kept in touch."

She paused a bit there. Glanced at Max. Like there was something she wanted to say to him, something she was holding back.

"Got a problem?"

"No," Aoife said. "It's just... well. Knowing what happened to your family. Kind of unsure whether I want to ask if you have any more family out there."

Max sighed. "Younger sister was a spoiled brat. Parents both dead."

"Any friends?"

Max frowned. "Do I look like the sort of guy who keeps friends?"

"Fair point."

They walked further, got closer to Max's house. And Max got the sense that there was a question in the air, lingering. An unasked question that Aoife wanted to raise.

A question he wanted her to delay because he wasn't sure how he was going to answer.

"Where you living now?" Max asked.

"A flat just outside of town. Live there with a few flatmates. I used to be in law, in another life. Gave it all up a few years back to pursue my dream of a zoology degree. Working in safari. Moving to some foreign country and just living with nature. That's kind of my dream. And it's the life my dad always wanted me to live, too. Before I got caught up in all the... noise."

Max heard Aoife's words, the way she was speaking, and he liked what he was hearing. She spoke the way he thought.

And it made him like her more.

But still, he couldn't ask the question.

He couldn't bring himself to do it.

"Come on," he said, looking away. "I'll show you around. You can... you can rest up here. For a bit."

She opened her mouth like she was going to protest. And then she smiled. Nodded. The unspoken question still unspoken.

"Sounds good."

Max opened the door to his house. Stepped inside. Kept his head down, barely wanting to look around because he knew it was a bit of a tip. But why would he tidy up? He only had himself to look after. Didn't have anyone else to think about.

"Wow," Aoife said, looking around with wide eyes. "Your place is... nice."

"Thanks," Max said, only realising how exhausted he was when he stepped through the door. "Come through to the kitchen. I've got a bit of food left over. About time we ate something."

He walked through to the kitchen when he noticed something.

His lounge door.

It was ajar.

He never left it ajar.

He stood there a few seconds. Stared at that crack in the door. His heart picked up. Adrenaline surged inside. He wasn't sure what it was. He couldn't explain it. But something felt wrong. Something just felt... *off*.

He pushed open the door to his lounge.

Someone was sitting there, on his leather sofa.

A figure that looked familiar.

A silhouette that looked familiar from long ago.

A silhouette he couldn't place.

But then that man turned around.

A smile stretched across his face.

And Max felt like he was back in the nightmares, all over again.

"Hello, Max," he said, as Rex growled beside him and Aoife. "Long time, no see."

CHAPTER THIRTY-NINE

Aoife saw the man sitting on the sofa, and her skin went cold.

Because she recognised him.

She recognised him immediately, and it made the hairs on the back of her neck stand on end.

She recognised him, and suddenly all the pieces of the puzzle clicked right into place.

The pieces she'd wanted to hide from.

The pieces she didn't want to admit.

But the pieces that were staring her right in the face.

"Hello, Max," the man said.

Max stood there. Totally still. But she could see his pupils dilating. She could see the anger in his eyes. See the pain on his face. She could see it all, and she understood. She understood profusely.

And then the man looked around at Aoife, looked right into her eyes.

For a moment, a pause.

For a moment, silence.

For a moment, total stillness.

And then, a smile across his face. "Wow," he said. "What *are* the chances?"

Aoife didn't know what to say. She couldn't speak. She felt tongue-tied. Frozen. The whole thing coming together in one aggressive dance.

And yet, she knew she should have known. She should have put the pieces of the puzzle together sooner.

Or maybe she had?

Maybe she had, and she was just hoping not to admit the truth?

Maybe that's the guilt that had drawn her to Max in the first place...

Something she found hard to admit.

But something she had to face up to.

Something she had to realise.

She looked at this man across the room, and her whole body went cold.

"Hello, sis," Seth said. "Long time, no see. How's things?"

CHAPTER FORTY

"Hello, sis," Seth said. "How's things?"

Max heard those words, and time stood still. Everything went cold.

Because he was filled with fear.

He was filled with rage.

He was filled with an urge—a need—for revenge.

And yet, he was frozen. Completely frozen and rooted to the spot.

He looked around at Aoife. "'Sis'?" he said.

Aoife looked around at him. Wide-eyed. "I'm sorry," she said. "I... I..."

"Did you know?"

"I wasn't sure. But I—"

"Did you know who I was?"

"Not at first. But when you said. About your family. I didn't want to believe it. But yes. I... I knew."

Max's fists tightened.

He felt a burning rage inside.

A burning desire for revenge.

He looked around at Seth, and he could only see one thing.

The man who killed his wife.

The man who killed his son.

He switched his attention from Aoife, still reeling from her betrayal, and he launched himself at Seth.

"I wouldn't," Seth said, standing and lifting a long, jagged-looking blade. "Not if you want to live."

Max stopped himself. It was the hardest thing to do. He wanted to keep going regardless. He wanted to batter Seth, even if it meant that blade buried between his ribs. He wanted to beat him to a pulp.

But it took all the resistance in the world to stop himself. To hold back. To resist.

Seth looked at him as he if was enjoying this. Smirked. "Good. Definitely the right choice."

"What the fuck are you doing in my home?"

Seth smiled. He walked from side to side, gripping that knife in his hand. "See, as you might've noticed, I got out of prison. Not a moment too soon, if you ask me. Like, it's okay in there. Decent. Far easier than you'd imagine. But I was bored. And I've spent all these years thinking about finishing the job I started all those years ago."

Max saw Kathryn in his mind's eye.

He saw David in his mind's eye.

He saw them both, and he felt sick.

He felt the truth emerging, once again.

"You made a mistake coming here," Max said.

"Max," Aoife said. "Be careful."

"Oh," Seth said, smirking. "Oh, be careful, huh? So you're with him now? That figures I guess. Seeing as you grassed on me. The cops arrived just when we were about to finish the job, right Max?"

Max thought back to that moment Seth stood in his house.

In David's bedroom.

How he was just about to launch his rage at this man, and

then the police came racing in.

"You warned the police," Max said.

Seth laughed. "See, my sister knew something was going to happen. But she was loyal. Loyal to a fault. Always Daddy's favourite for a reason."

Max looked around at Aoife. Saw the tears rolling down her cheeks.

"I knew something was wrong when he visited me. I... I followed him. And then I—I rang them."

"You knew something was going to happen."

Aoife shook her head. "If I'd known how bad it was going to be... I would've acted sooner. I just had a bad feeling. But I didn't know."

"You had a chance to stop him. And because you didn't... my family died."

Aoife opened her mouth.

But no words came out.

And in that instant, Max felt nothing but hate for the pair of them.

"Apple doesn't fall far from the tree," Seth said. "That's the truth. Whether we like to admit it or not."

"I'm nothing like you," Aoife spat.

Seth laughed. "But you are. Because it's like you said. You could've done more. But hey. Max here could've done more too, am I right?"

Max gritted his teeth.

Felt the memory creeping back into his consciousness.

He didn't want to think about it.

He didn't want to dwell on it.

He didn't want to go down that road again.

"Don't," Max said, tightening his fists.

"I remember the way he squealed," Seth said. "The way you came storming into the bedroom."

"Stop!"

"And the way I held his knife to his neck, and the way you froze."

He said those words, and the bottom fell out of Max's world, right in an instant.

Because what Seth said was true.

As much as he tried to tell himself there was nothing he could do to save David... he was wrong.

Because David had been alive when Max entered the bedroom.

His son had stared into his dad's eyes as Seth held the knife to his neck.

Max froze in fear. He froze in trying to be diplomatic. In trying to save him in some other way.

And then he cut David's throat right before him.

"You took everything away from me," Seth said. "My girlfriend, Sandy. Remember her? The only time I'd ever fallen in love, and you took her from me. You took my life away from me. So now, it's your turn. I've haunted you for years. And now it's finally time to meet your end."

Max gritted his teeth. Lost in thought. Unable to speak. Not sure what to say. Not sure what to do.

"Max," Aoife said. "Don't do this. Don't do what he wants you to do."

But he didn't hear Aoife anymore.

He didn't hear anything.

He just felt his grief, his pain, and his desire for revenge.

And then he launched himself at Seth.

Seth stepped back, casually as ever.

He lifted that knife.

And he buried it into Max's side.

Max felt a burning hot bolt of pain as Rex barked somewhere behind him.

He heard a shout. Aoife.

He felt that rage, and he wanted to stand up, he wanted to

fight, he wanted to take this man down.

But all he could do was look up at him as his legs shook, as the knife stuck into him.

Seth standing there, smirking.

"I've waited a long time for this," he said.

And then he pulled the knife out of Max, and as much as Max wanted to be strong, he fell to the floor.

He hit the floor with his knees.

He gripped his side. Bleeding out. Head spinning. In agony.

Seth stood over him. Walked around him, knife in hand. Smile on his face.

"And now you'll die alone," he said.

He walked around Max. Patted him on the head, then pushed him to the wooden floor.

And behind, Max saw Aoife standing there. Tears falling down her face. Hands in front of her mouth.

Seth walked over to her.

Stood right in front of her.

"We've got some unfinished business, too, sis."

"Seth—"

He grabbed her arm.

Held the blade to her neck.

And then, as Rex stood there, kicking back, barking, he watched as Seth dragged her out of the lounge, screaming out, crying.

Seth looked back at Max.

Right into his eyes.

Smiled.

"Goodbye, Max. It's been a pleasure. Really."

He slammed the living room door shut.

Max tried to clamber his way to his feet.

Then he felt a large bolt of pain right through the side of his body.

And he collapsed to the floor, and everything went dark.

CHAPTER FORTY-ONE

Max lay on the floor of his lounge and felt the pain splitting through his body.

The morning sun shone in through the windows, right onto his face. But he felt cold. Freezing cold, right to the bone. Kept on shivering, shaking. Teeth rattling together.

Because he couldn't believe what had just happened.

What had just transpired in a matter of moments.

Walking into his home.

Finding Seth here.

The man who murdered his wife and son.

Finding out Aoife was Seth's sister.

Finding out she knew he was going to do something bad but wasn't able to stop him.

And then the lust for revenge growing too strong for Max to resist, as he launched himself at Seth and the knife buried into his side.

He turned onto his side, but his whole body hurt. He could see blood trickling from a stab wound in his right. It looked bad. Not ridiculously deep, and fortunately, he didn't seem to be leaking too much blood. Hopefully, he'd got lucky. Hopefully, hadn't hit any major organs or arteries. But still bad.

He knew he could stitch it up. Clean it up. Dress and bandage it. And he knew he had the capability to do so as a former army medic.

But there was another question in his mind.

A question of whether it was even worth it anymore.

He lay there on the floor and tightened his fists. The memory of what Seth told him circling his mind.

Rushing into David's bedroom.

Finding Seth with a blade to his throat.

Smile across his face.

"Come on. It's not too late to save him."

Freezing.

Wanting to throw himself at that man.

Wanting to tear him from his son.

But at the same time, staring into his son's eyes and feeling so terrified.

Not wanting him to suffer.

Not wanting him to die.

So turning to diplomacy.

"Please," he said. "Don't hurt him. Please."

Seeing Seth's smile widen.

Hearing him laugh.

And knowing right then that he'd made the wrong instinctive choice.

"Too late," Seth said.

And then he sliced David's throat.

The rest was a blur.

Max launching himself towards David.

Cradling him in his arms.

And then the anger. The anger as the police arrived before he could do anything to punish Seth.

The rage.

Wanting to make him pay for what he'd done in that grief-stricken state.

But not being able to.

Seth, arrested.

Max, alone.

He rolled over onto his back, and he stared up at his lounge ceiling. A cold breeze blew in through the front door, making him shiver.

And then he saw the dog standing there, staring at him.

His immediate reaction and instinct were of disgust. Because this dog was Aoife's. He associated it with her. And she'd betrayed him.

And he felt an idiot. He felt a dick. Because he'd allowed himself to open up. Allowed himself to actually prematurely *feel* something about somebody, even though he barely knew her. Got caught up in all the sentimental shit. The same sentimental shit that'd got him nothing but pain in the past.

And now she was gone.

Not only gone, but she wasn't who he thought she was.

She was Seth's sister. And she knew exactly who Max was all along.

He thought about the story. How she was worried about him. How she followed him. And how she called the police on him, but not early enough.

She could've stopped this.

Aoife could've stopped Kathryn and David's deaths.

But she hadn't.

And now they were gone.

He looked at the dog, and he saw nothing but Aoife in its big brown eyes.

"Go," Max said.

Rex tilted his head. Whimpered a little.

"I said get out of here!" Max shouted.

The dog backed away, just a little. But he was still here. Still standing there. Still staring. Like there was something he could do to help.

And Max felt so lost. He felt so afraid. And he felt so guilty, too. So guilty for so many things.

And so helpless, as he clutched his stabbed side, blood trickling through his fingertips.

There was nothing he could do to even get this dog away.

There was nothing he could do to fight through the reminders of the past. Of his failures.

Nothing at all.

He clutched onto his side, rolled over, and closed his eyes.

The dog panted by his side.

He wanted to tell it to go.

Wanted to shout at it to get the hell away from here.

But all he could do was lie there in the cold, shivering away, and squeeze his eyes shut.

Alone.

CHAPTER FORTY-TWO

Aoife tried to wrestle herself free from her brother, but to no avail.

He always was the stronger one, physically. It used to annoy her no end. She always wanted to be the stronger one, especially as she was definitely the cleverer one. It used to bug her that for all her intelligence over Seth, he physically overwhelmed her all the time.

It annoyed her too because she knew there was a dark side to her big brother. A side nobody wanted to acknowledge. Not her. Not Dad. Nobody.

But a side that was there, and a side that was always going to erupt, eventually.

She remembered the time she caught him plucking at the wings of a fly, fascinated grin on his face. Or the time she found him holding a local cat by the tail when he was a little bit older. He had a sick sense of humour. Seemed to like pinching her. Punching her a little harder than was comfortable for play fighting.

And there were other things, too. Locking her in the boot of a car. Telling her it was light in there. That the light stayed on at all times, and that she didn't have to worry.

She remembered when the light went off. When the darkness descended. She remembered screaming and screaming for what felt like hours. Weeing herself. Giving up hope as tears stung her cheeks. Screaming until her voice went hoarse.

And it was only later when Dad finally got to the car that he figured out what'd happened.

He bollocked Seth. Truly bollocked him.

Dad always saw through him. Always saw him for what he was. *He's a problem, that kid,* Aoife would overhear him saying to his girlfriend at the time, Annabelle. *He's going to bring us nothing but trouble.*

And as Aoife felt Seth's hand around her neck, tight, dragging her away from Max's house, she realised Dad was so right in that instant.

She looked back at Max's house, and she felt a sense of shame. She'd had a feeling he was the one whose family her brother had killed three years ago. Some of the things he said just added up.

But she hadn't wanted to rub it in his face or anything. And there'd even been an element of denial, too. A sense that if she didn't acknowledge the past, she wouldn't have to think about it.

But there was only so long you could run from the past.

There was only so long you could hide from the truth.

She thought of the day Seth came to visit her. They drifted even more than they already had in their teens and twenties. Didn't see much of each other. Aoife thought he was trouble, so she didn't want much to do with him.

She remembered him turning up that evening. The way she walked into her flat after working a case on an overturned dangerous driving situation for a woman with diminished responsibility on the grounds of mental health and found him sitting there already.

"How did you get in?"

Seth looked around at her, sipping a whisky. "Key under the doormat. Rookie error."

"Well," Aoife said. "I've had a busy day, so I won't be staying up too late."

"Don't worry. I just thought I'd come see you. Not sure when I'll be seeing you again."

She remembered those words and the sense of foreboding they instilled in her. The feeling that something was wrong. Because it wasn't characteristic of Seth to say something like that.

And Aofie couldn't shake the overriding sense that he was going to do something bad.

But what did she do about it?

Nothing.

Not until it was too late.

She followed him. Went out looking for him. Already wondering if she should call the police.

But what would she say? *I'm worried about my brother. I don't know where he is or what he's doing, but he creeps me out a bit.*

She remembered seeing him walk into that house.

Remembered standing there for a while and him not stepping out of it.

And it only being later on when she'd finally bit the bullet and trusted her gut and called the police. Told them she had a bad feeling. That something terrible was going to happen at that address.

An intuition she couldn't rationally explain.

She remembered seeing the headlines. The double murder of a woman and child. A revenge killing for the girlfriend of her brother being locked away.

And she remembered the guilt she'd felt. The guilt that would haunt her forever.

She could've done more.

She could've acted.

The guilt drove her out of law and into new pursuits.

So many lives were changed in that instant.

She felt the pain around her neck tighten for just a moment, and then she collapsed to the ground.

Seth stood over her. She could see him smiling at her. That smug smile, that malicious grin, one she was so familiar with.

"What do you want with me?" she gasped.

Seth laughed. Shook his head. "Funny thing to say to your brother who you haven't seen in three years."

"Seth—"

"Shush," he said. "Now's not the time for talking. But I'm going to need you to stop wriggling."

Aoife clambered onto her knees. Stood up. Stared right into his eyes. "Well, that's not going to happen."

Seth sighed. "Shame, sis. Shame. I really didn't want to have to do this."

Aoife frowned. "What—"

And then she felt a punch.

A heavy punch right across her face.

And in an instant, she fell to the ground again.

Tasted blood in her mouth.

Right in the back of her throat.

She looked around. Looked up into the blurry haze above, where her brother stood over her.

"Sorry," he said. "It's nothing personal."

And then he pulled back his foot, buried it into her face, and everything went black.

CHAPTER FORTY-THREE

One moment, Max was in the darkness.
    The next, he saw light.
    He was driving home. Driving home from work. He felt younger. More sprightly. More optimistic. More... *happy*.

And it felt strange. Because he'd been here. He'd been here before. Only the last few times he'd been here, he was concerned. He was worried. He was terrified.

Because he knew exactly what trauma he was heading towards.

He knew he was going to find something terrible back at his house.

But right now... he didn't have that feeling.

He drove up to his drive. Pulled onto it. He got out, and he stood in front of the front door.

And right away, he noticed what was different about this to the other times he'd been here.

He saw the light in the kitchen.

And he saw someone walking around in there.

A momentary sense of dread. Someone was in the house. Someone was in the house, and they were going to hurt Kathryn. They were going to hurt David.

He rushed to the door, put the key in the lock, and turned it. Stepped inside, hurried into the kitchen.

And right away, he saw her.

She was glowing. Glowing in a way that looked angelic.

He looked around for a sign that she was in danger. A sign that she was hurt. A sign that she was in pain.

But the more he looked, the more he didn't find any of those signs.

Because she was okay.

Kathryn stood before him.

His wife stood before him.

Dark hair.

Bright blue eyes.

Beaming smile.

"Hello, Max. What took you so long?"

Max stood there before her, and he felt this deep, overwhelming sense of sadness. The overwhelming sense of grief. Because he knew he wasn't really here. He knew Kathryn wasn't really here.

But it looked so real. It felt so real. Crystal clear as day.

"Why don't you sit down?" she asked. "Look like you've had a long day."

He looked around, over towards David's room. He could see light coming from that room. And he still felt a sense of fear. He still felt a sense of dread. Because he'd been here before, and he'd been here so many times, enough times to know that good things did not await.

"David," he said.

"David's okay," Kathryn said. "He's just playing on his Xbox."

"But..."

"He's okay," Kathryn said, planting a hand on Max's arm. "He's okay, Max. Trust me."

He turned around and looked at Kathryn, and once again, he felt that sadness. Because on the one hand, it felt so nice to feel her touch against his skin. It lit up every inch of his body with flames of happiness, joy, love.

But on the other hand... it was so long since he'd last felt this way.

And it made him realise even more how much he missed it.

How much he craved it.

How much he craved *her*.

How much he craved the life he'd lost.

He sat down, trusting his wife. And she sat down right before him. Right in front of him.

Sat there and smiled at him.

"This is weird, isn't it?" she said.

"What... what is this?"

Kathryn reached for his hand again. "And once again, he felt like fireworks were exploding inside him when she touched him.

"It's the place where you remember," she said.

"Remember what?"

"Never to give up on people."

He heard those words, and again, he tasted a sickliness in his mouth. Felt the guilt inside. Because he had given up on people. He felt it overwhelm him in an instant. And it was painful. It hurt. A lot.

He'd turned his back on everyone.

Because he was so afraid of what bonding with people might bring.

What connecting with people might bring.

But maybe that was the wrong way.

Maybe that was the wrong approach all along.

"I've tried," Max said.

"And I believe you. I've seen it. But... but Max, you need to learn to forgive yourself."

"How can I forgive myself?"

"Because it wasn't your fault. None of it was your fault."

He heard those words, and against all his instincts, he did something he hadn't done in a long time.

He cried.

Kathryn wrapped her arms around him.

"You did what you thought was right at the moment."

"I could've fought for him—"

"And Seth would've taken his life anyway, and you would still have blamed yourself. You didn't do this, Max. You didn't do any of this. None of this is on you. But you have a choice now. You have a choice."

He moved his head away. Looked into Kathryn's bright blue eyes. The whole scene around her was glowing, angelic.

"What choice?"

"You can come with David and me, and you can give up. Or you can try again. You can try again, and you can join us when you're ready. When you're *truly* ready. Only you know what that entails."

In an instant, instinctively, Max knew his answer. "Then I'll join you and David. I'm—I'm ready."

Kathryn's face turned. A look of... was it disappointment?

"Are you sure you are ready?"

"I've been ready since the day you went away."

"But are you *truly* ready? Or is there something you'd like to do, still? Something you'd like to... achieve?"

He went to open his mouth, and then he saw her. He saw Aoife right before him. He saw Seth dragging her away.

He felt his anger towards her. The sense that he'd been betrayed.

And then he heard what she'd said.

That she was sorry.

That she didn't know what he could've done.

That she wished she'd acted sooner.

He heard all these things, all these protestations, and then

Aoife disappeared, and suddenly he was back with Kathryn again, and she was standing between two doors.

Both of them had light underneath.

Both of them were the same, dark wood.

But Max knew the choice he was faced with right away.

"You get to choose," Kathryn said. "And it is your choice. It is truly your choice. But you go through the left door, and you join me and David. Or you go through the right, and you finish what deep down you know you still have to finish. What you have to achieve."

He heard her words, and he cried. Because he didn't want to leave her. She seemed so real, felt so real, and he didn't want to leave her behind. Not again.

But then there was that other sense inside him.

The sense that there *was* unfinished business.

That there *were* things he still needed to attend to. Still needed to address.

"I don't want to leave you," he said.

Kathryn smiled. "You aren't leaving me. And I'm not going anywhere. Neither is David. We'll be here. Right here. For whenever you're ready."

Max walked up to the two doors.

He stood between them both.

He looked into Kathryn's eyes, and then he leaned in, and he kissed her, and it felt like he was drifting away, right back to the first time they'd met on the beach.

"I'll come back for you," he said.

"And I won't go anywhere. Neither will David."

He took a deep breath. Nodded. "I love you."

"I love you too, Max. So much."

He turned away from her.

Turned towards the door ahead of him.

The door back to his life.

He looked at Kathryn one last time and saw her smiling.

"Go on," she said. "Go do what you need to do."

He nodded.

Took a deep breath.

And then, before he could change his mind, he stepped through the door into the light.

* * *

Max opened his eyes.

CHAPTER FORTY-FOUR

Max opened his eyes, and right away, he knew what he needed to do.

It was light in his house. Sunlight peeking in through the windows. The air was cold, and he was shivering like mad. But for some reason, it didn't bother him. He didn't care.

Because what mattered was what he had to do.

He turned around and felt a sharp pain, right along the right side of his torso.

He looked down. Saw blood still trickling from the wound on his side. His mouth was dry. He felt sick. He knew he must've passed out, but he wasn't sure for how long.

Just that there was still time.

There was still a chance.

He heard panting.

Looked around.

Saw the dog, Rex, staring at him and wagging his tail.

Instinctively, Max wanted to tell him to go away. Because that dog didn't want to be anywhere near him. Not with his track record.

But then he heard that voice as just noise in his mind.

And he heard Kathryn's words.

Felt her hand against him.

Finish what you know you have to finish. We're not going anywhere.

He looked at Rex, took a deep breath, and he sighed.

"Alright, lad?"

Rex wandered over to him. He nudged his head against his hand, which he weirdly kind of liked and appreciated.

"Good lad. Good lad. Alright, now. Give me some space. Need to figure out how we're gonna go about this."

He knew it was going to be painful standing up. But really, he had no choice. He wasn't lying on the floor of his lounge and accepting his fate. He was getting the hell up, and he was sorting his wound out.

Then, he could think about the next step.

He gritted his teeth. Pulled himself to his feet, using the back of his sofa to support himself. He felt dizzy. Lightheaded. Weak.

He felt that urge to return to the dream, to the vision.

To return to the room Kathryn had given him the opportunity to join her in.

And then he pushed that thought aside.

He looked around the room. Looked over towards his kitchen, where he'd have plenty of supplies gathered.

He staggered over there, in pain, wincing with every step. Fully aware that he might just collapse at any moment, especially with how dizzy he felt.

But he gritted his teeth and walked over there anyway, Rex by his side at all times, shadowing him in every moment.

And as much as Max didn't want to admit it, he liked the company.

It made him feel like he wasn't alone here.

Even though that in itself made him feel somewhat vulnerable.

He ignored that vulnerability and walked into the kitchen area. He searched the shelves for supplies he knew he had.

Supplies he could help. Blood trickling onto the floor all the time as he clutched his side, applying pressure to the wound.

He scavenged his way through the kitchen, then down into the cellar under his house, until he found some alcohol to clean the wound. Some stitches to stop it bleeding. He had all sorts of medical shit down here. Enough stuff to make a bloody intravenous drip if he needed to. Not that he ever bloody would need to.

He bandaged himself up. It might not be ideal. It probably wouldn't help. And he was an infection risk.

But he was in a far, far better position than he was before, and that was something.

He stood there. Rex by his side, staring up at him. He felt a little shaky. A little weak. And in a lot of pain.

But he knew what he had to do.

He knew exactly what he had to do.

He grabbed a hunting rifle.

He walked over to the door to his house.

Looked outside and took a deep breath of the crisp January air.

Looked at the footprints where Seth had walked.

Where he'd taken Aoife.

And then he took another deep breath and tightened his fists.

"Come on, lad," he said to Rex. "Let's go get Aoife back."

CHAPTER FORTY-FIVE

Seth stared across the cabin at Aoife, and he wasn't sure how to feel about his long-lost sister.

He'd never liked her all that much. But then he supposed some would say he'd never liked *anyone* all that much. Other than Sandy, anyway. Something different about her. Ever since he first met her, he always sensed they were similar. That they were cut from the same cloth. That they understood each other.

He wondered where she would be now if she hadn't taken her life in prison. He wondered where the pair of them would be now. If they'd be living some kind of ordinary life. A life Seth never envisaged or fancied before he met her, but a life that did seem growingly appealing the more he'd got to know her.

He sighed. He didn't want to think about the life he could've had. The life that was taken away from him.

He could only think about the people who'd taken everything away from him.

One of those being Max.

He looked over his shoulder, away from the derelict little cabin he'd found. Through the cracked, grimy window. Max was far behind. He'd be bleeding out right now. Dying slowly and alone on the floor of his home.

And as much as Seth wanted to be there to witness his every struggle... there was a part of him that was happy that he'd subjected him to the loneliness to die.

A part of him that knew that's exactly the way Max wouldn't want to go out.

Just that dog beside him.

A dog that would do a runner for it if it had any sense.

He heard a groan and turned around.

Aoife was awake. Squinting. She had a big red bump on her head. He had her tied to a stool.

"What..." she said, looking around, disoriented. Looking around this dark wood cabin. Mould and moss everywhere. The smell of damp pervasive and strong. "Where am..."

She saw Seth, and her eyes widened.

That fear.

That same look of fear she'd had in her eyes when they were kids. When he'd chase her with a knife. Or when he'd push her down the stairs but hold on to her, tormenting her.

Maybe he did like Aoife, after all.

Just not for the reasons you probably should like your sister.

"Seth," she said, blood trickling down her chin. He could tell she was trying to do her strong voice, but he could also tell she was afraid. She struggled, pulled against the ties around her wrists, around her ankles. "Let me the hell out of here. Right this second."

Seth smirked. Shook his head. "Never learned, did you, sis? When did I ever just *let* you out of anything?"

"This isn't a game."

"You're too right. It's not a game. It's very, very serious business."

"I don't know what you want, but you aren't going to get it from me."

"You still don't see it, do you?" Seth said, shaking his head. "All this time, and you still don't get it."

"If this is about what happened three years ago, then I'm not sorry. Not one bit. My only regret is that I didn't ring the police earlier."

"But you didn't, did you? And that's on you. And now your new little boyfriend knows exactly what you are. And that's what he'll die knowing. That someone else had a chance to help him. That they hesitated. And that they betrayed him."

"You are a piece of shit," Aoife spat. "You're a piece of shit, and you're a sad excuse of a brother. Dad always knew—"

"Dad knew jack shit," Seth spat. "He always favoured you. His little princess."

"That's because he knew what you were."

Seth smiled. "And what am I, Aoife?"

He saw his sister staring back at him. And he didn't like the defiance in her eyes.

He stood up.

Walked over to her.

"What am I?"

"You're a monster."

He chuckled. Shook his head. "That's exactly what Dad said, you know? The last thing he said to me, in fact."

Aoife frowned. "What?"

"Before I pushed him down the stairs. I looked him in the eyes after he'd caught me stealing from Mum's old jewellery box. Well, *borrowing*. And he told me he was going to tell the police and the rest of our family everything. The diamond necklace Mum inherited. I needed some cash. And she never looked at it anyway. She wouldn't want me suffering or struggling."

"I don't... I don't understand. Dad... Dad died of a heart attack. He—"

"He caught me," Seth said. "He threatened to tell people. To tell the police. He got to the top of the stairs, and... well. Let's just say he regretted it."

He saw his sister's eyes widen. Saw the tears well up. Saw the panic and the confusion spread across her face.

"You—you killed Dad?"

"I killed Dad," Seth said. "I didn't want to tell you because I guess you've always idolised him, haven't you? And I really, really didn't want to cause any sour grapes between us. But then you rang the police on me. You stopped me from punishing Max three years ago, fully. And you never once visited me. You left me to rot in there. You didn't even tell me Auntie Carol had died. I had to find out from the chaplain. You abandoned me. And then I find you with *him* of all people. How poetic. How... disgusting."

He saw his sister shaking her head. Crying. "You killed him." She was clearly fixated on this point. "You—you killed Dad. You monster. You fucking animal. You murderous—"

He smacked her across the face then, shutting her up.

But it didn't work.

She kicked out. Shook. Tried to break free, even though she didn't have a chance.

And all Seth did was stand there and watch her have her hysterics, have her little tantrum.

"That's it," he said. "Get it all out. Get all the whinging and moaning out."

"I'll kill you."

Seth laughed. "You what?"

"I said I'll... I'll kill you."

"A night without power, and that's what you've become? You really expect me to believe that? Besides. You wouldn't stand a chance even if you wanted to. Not tied up like this."

He looked at his sister, and he saw her like he used to see the flies he pulled wings off.

The spiders he'd pluck legs from.

And then he walked to the back of the cabin, and he grabbed a machete.

"No, you aren't killing me," he said. "But I can't make the same promise to you."

He walked right over to Aoife.

Machete in hand.

Heart racing.

Shaking with adrenaline.

And was that an erection he felt?

It'd been so long.

So, so long.

"Any last words?" he said. "Because you like to speak, don't you? To the police. To Max. To so, so many."

She spat at him.

"Rot in hell, you piece of shit."

He wiped the thick green blob of phlegm from his shirt.

And then he shook his head.

"If that's all."

And then he reached for her mouth.

Yanked her tongue out.

Placed his machete against it as she shook her head, tried to bite his fingers, shouted out.

And Seth stood over her, and he smiled.

"Time to put an end to your speaking, sis."

He lifted the machete.

Aoife screamed.

CHAPTER FORTY-SIX

Max walked through the woods by his house, Rex by his side, and followed Seth and Aoife's trails.

It was an icy cold morning. Really bright, really sunny. He always loved getting up early when he was off work, wandering in the woods, disappearing into nature. He really felt at home in nature more than anything, especially when he was totally alone.

Weirdly, it made him feel more connected with the world around him. Like that's how he got his sense of connection. That's where he derived it from. From the world, not from other people.

But that was starting to take on a different meaning now.

Especially now he was searching for Aoife.

He followed the footsteps on the ground. He was good at tracking. An old army trick he'd learned back in the day. But this wasn't difficult to follow. Seth clearly wasn't clever or forward-thinking enough to cover his tracks right now.

Especially in the heat of the moment.

But Max worried. Worried what Seth might've done to Aoife.

Even though his feelings on Aoife were understandably mixed.

He walked on, gritting his teeth, limping as his side ached with pain, not as quick as he could usually move. Aoife had let him down. She could've called the police earlier. She could've given the authorities a heads up before Seth did anything. Before he killed Kathryn. David.

But then he figured *he* could've come home earlier when Kathryn didn't text him that day, too.

He figured *he* could've acted faster and maybe saved Little David's life.

There were so many variables. But at the end of the day... he truly believed Aoife regretted not acting sooner. He knew regret far too well.

And her brother was a psychopathic fucker who was going to regret the day he ever crossed Max. Regret the day he ever turned up in his life again.

And regret the day he dragged his sister off into the wilderness.

He gripped onto his hunting rifle. It felt alien. Like he was back in the military. The adjustment to a life where he was carrying a hunting rifle around in public... it was going to be hard to adapt to. Hard to adjust to.

But then it seemed like the power still hadn't returned. So it wasn't going to be long before the brittle legs society was propped up on collapsed once and for all.

He took a few further steps into the woods when he noticed something and stopped.

There were footprints right below him. The same footprints he'd followed for quite some time now.

Only there was something else beside those footprints.

Something that sent a shiver up Max's spine.

Something that looked like blood.

Rex whimpered. Panted. Looked ahead.

And Max looked down the slope and ahead into the distance, too.

"I know, lad," he said. "I know. But we've just gotta keep on going. I'm sure she'll be okay. I'm..."

That's when Max heard something that sent a shiver up his spine.

Right down the hill, he heard a scream.

Aoife's scream.

CHAPTER FORTY-SEVEN

Seth went to press the blade down into Aoife's tongue when something caught his eye.
 It was outside the window of the dark cabin he was in. A glimpse of movement up the hills.

Aoife let out this pitiful scream that reminded him of when they were kids, and when he used to taunt her and tease her and try to toughen her the hell up, and it sent a shiver down his spine.

But then he turned around, her tongue still between his fingers, and he looked outside.

That's when he saw him.

Limping down the slope.

Limping towards the cabin.

That dog by his side.

And he felt torn. A combination of emotions. Because, on the one hand, he was infuriated. This wasn't how it was supposed to go. Max wasn't supposed to be alive still. He was supposed to be dead. He was supposed to die alone.

But on the other hand…

He couldn't help admiring him.

Admiring him for dragging himself out of the pit Seth had left him in.

That showed character.

That showed strength.

And Seth kind of liked that.

He watched him limp towards the cabin, and he smiled.

He turned around to Aoife.

Saw her staring out the window, too. Tears staining her cheeks. But a look of defiance on her face.

A look he knew he needed to wipe away.

He reached into his pocket. Grabbed the gag he'd used earlier. And as Aoife kicked and shook and struggled, he tied that gag around her mouth. Tight.

And then he put a hand on her shoulder.

Looked into her eyes and smiled.

"Don't worry," Seth said. "You'll be just fine here."

And then, before Max and the dog could make it here, he turned around from Aoife, stepped out of the cabin.

He saw the old petrol canisters by the cabin, and he smiled.

He knew exactly what he had to do.

CHAPTER FORTY-EIGHT

Max heard the scream, and he knew he couldn't hesitate.

It was Aoife. She was up ahead somewhere, right in the distance.

And it sounded like she was suffering.

It sounded like she was in pain.

In danger.

Or worse.

He gritted his teeth, and he heard Rex growl beside him. Let out a little bark.

And he knew he couldn't delay in any way.

He ran. Ran as fast as his weak, stabbed body would allow. It ached. Sent crippling, shooting pains right through his body.

And he knew he was being reckless. He knew he should be careful. He knew he should slow down. Not rush a thing.

Because he was going to end up hurting himself.

But hearing that scream. It created a sense of urgency in him. A sense that he needed to do something. He needed to act. Fast.

So he ran down the slope, through the trees.

And that's when he saw it.

Up ahead. A cabin. A cabin he'd seen many times. Even sheltered in there once when he was out and got caught in a storm.

Wasn't nice in there. Wasn't ideal at all. Grimy. Dusty. Not the sort of place you wanted to get holed up in.

But looking down the slope, looking at this cabin, and looking at the footsteps and the specks of blood leading right down towards it... Max knew immediately this was exactly where he had to go.

"Come on, lad," he said.

He limped down the slope as quickly as he could. He hadn't heard another scream, and that worried him.

Because if Aoife only screamed once, what did that mean?

What had happened?

He walked down the slope, and he felt like he was heading towards David's room again, three years ago. He felt like he was going to open that cabin door and find Seth standing there, a blade to Aoife's throat.

Or find Aoife sitting there in a heap, blood spilling out of her stomach, just like Kathryn.

He thought of the guilt he'd felt back then. He thought of the guilt he'd feel if that happened again.

He thought about it all.

And then he thought about the vision of Kathryn he'd had when he'd passed out on his living room floor.

The way she'd looked at him.

The things she'd said to him.

Finish what you know you have to finish. We're not going anywhere.

He remembered these words, and he felt a sudden weight lift from his shoulders.

A sudden assurance about what he had to do.

He tightened his fists.

"I'm coming," he said.

And then he staggered down the slope, right towards the cabin.

As he got to the cabin, he couldn't see anyone in there. And the door. It looked ajar.

He suddenly noticed something.

Rex.

Rex wasn't beside him.

Rex was right behind him. Looking around, tilting his head either side.

"Rex?" Max said.

But Rex was preoccupied. Something was holding his attention.

"Rex," Max said. "Come on."

Rex looked around at him, the cold wind blowing against the trees. Everything so quiet. So silent. Too silent.

He turned around the cabin.

Stepped up the rickety wooden steps, which were rotting away.

Reached the door.

And for a moment, he froze.

Do you want to go in there?

Do you really want to go in there?

He took a deep breath.

Swallowed a lump in his throat.

And then he pushed the door open.

It took his eyes a moment to adjust to what he was looking at.

But when he saw, he understood in an instant.

Aoife was sitting on the opposite side of the cabin.

She was bound.

Gagged.

And she was shaking her head.

Staring at Max with wide, tearful eyes and shaking her head.

"Come on," Max said. "Let's... let's get you..."

First, he noticed the strong stench of petrol, and he knew something was wrong.

And then he heard the footsteps creaking behind him.

He heard it before he saw him.

He heard the door creaking shut.

He spun around.

Saw Seth at the window.

Smile on his face.

And a lighter in his hand.

"Good luck getting out of this one," he said.

And then he threw a match inside the cabin, and the flames erupted.

CHAPTER FORTY-NINE

Max felt the flames igniting right away, and he knew he was in deep shit.

The first thing he did was launch himself towards the door. The door that Seth had just slammed shut. He bashed his side against it, which hurt, especially hurting the right side, which was stabbed, and hurt like mad.

But he kept on going and going because he couldn't just accept he was burning in here.

He couldn't let himself Aoife and Rex die in here.

Especially not at the hands of Seth.

But the more he banged against it, the more he realised there was no hope.

There was no getting out of that door.

Whatever Seth had put in front of it had stopped it from moving at all.

He looked around. Saw Aoife still sitting there, eyes wide, gagged, and cuffed. Saw Rex backing away from the growing flames, kicking at the broken wooden floor, barking. Saw smoke rising right away. And he knew he didn't have any time to mess around. Not now.

He ran over to Aoife, past the flames, which were already hot. He pulled the gag off her, and she coughed, spluttered.

"I thought you were dead," she said.

"I'm here."

"I'm sorry. I'm sorry about—"

"We can speak about that when we get out of here."

He checked the ties on her wrists, her ankles. Pulled against them. But they were tight. Ridiculously tight.

"I need to find something to cut these with."

He looked around the room, looked for something he could use.

And then it came to him.

The knife.

The hunting knife. Becker BK2. Favourite kind of knife and one he treasured, even though owning knives wasn't exactly legal over here.

He pulled it out of his pocket with his shaking hand.

Sliced away the ties, one by one.

And then when Aoife went to stand, the moment she went to stand, Max heard something behind.

The flames. They were breaking the damp wood already.

The route towards the door was shrinking by the second.

"We don't have much time here," Max said. "Come on."

He ran over to the other side of the room, past the flames.

But Rex didn't join them.

He stayed by the side of the chair where Aoife was tied, and he growled.

"Rex," Max said. "Come on."

But Rex stayed put.

Max gritted his teeth. "I'm not leaving you behind, goddammit."

He ran past the flames again, which were growing.

He tried to push Rex along, but he wouldn't budge.

"I can't... I can't make him," Max said.

"Rex, come on," Aoife said.

But Rex didn't move.

And Max found history repeating itself again.

He knew how this went down.

He knew what happened next.

But then he found himself standing against that thought.

He found himself resisting.

"No," he said. "It doesn't have to be that way."

He crouched down. It was already really smoky in here. So smoky he was coughing, which just hurt his stabbed side even more.

He put a hand on Rex's back. Rex, who panted away, tongue dangling out from between his teeth.

"Come on, lad," Max said. "It's okay. I know you've been through some stuff. But you can trust me. You can... you can do this."

He knew his words were falling on deaf ears. Rex was a dog, after all.

And he could see the fear in Rex's eyes. The way his ears went back. The way his docked little tail stayed plastered to his back end.

He was about to give up and walk away when Rex ran along to Aoife's side.

"Rex," she said, smiling. "Good boy. Good boy."

Max ran along with her. He went to run through the fire when he stopped.

Because it was already too late.

The flames were too big.

There was no way he was getting through them unscathed.

He looked over at Aoife.

Aoife looked back at him.

That knowing recognition in her eyes.

"Max?"

Max opened his mouth. And as he stood there, as he stared,

he saw that Aoife was still stuck. He saw that Rex was still stuck. He saw the pair of them were still trapped and that he couldn't let them die like this.

Because he recognised exactly why he'd come back now.

When he'd stood at that door and chosen which door to go through, he knew exactly what Kathryn meant when she said his work wasn't done.

"Max, quick," Aoife said. "You can make it. You can still make it."

But Max took a deep breath.

And sincerely, honestly, he smiled.

"You need to go. And you need to go back to my cabin. You'll find everything you need there. The rest... you'll figure it out along the way. Because you're smart."

Aoife shook her head. "Max? No. Don't give up. Don't—"

"Go," Max said. "You did everything you could for me. And I owe you... I owe you a thank you. For making me realise."

"Realise what?" Aoife asked. Tearful.

"For making me realise there was more left to live for."

He lifted his rifle.

He pointed at the window.

And he pulled the trigger.

The glass smashed.

And Aoife and Rex had a chance.

"Push Rex through. Then get out of there."

"But—"

"Before it's too late."

Aoife stood there, paralysed. Shaking her head. And Max saw himself in her.

"Don't see it as leaving me behind," he said. "You've saved me in ways you don't even realise. But you have to get out of here. And you have to get Rex out of here. Now."

She opened her mouth. Tried to speak.

And then she shook her head.

"I'm sorry."

"Don't be sorry."

"For everything. I'm—"

"Don't be sorry."

She looked back at him.

And through the smoke, through the flames, through Max's burning tears, he swore he saw a young Kathryn in her eyes.

"Go. Now. Now!"

She turned around.

Dragged Rex towards the window, lifting his slight weight and pushing him through.

"Thank God you're underweight right now," she spluttered.

Then she climbed the side of the cabin wall.

Turned around, one last time.

She looked at him. Looked right into his eyes as the heat grew more intense, as the smoke grew thicker.

"I'm sorry."

And Max just smiled, and he nodded.

"I'm sorry too."

And then Aoife turned around and climbed out of the window.

Max stood in the flames.

He stood in the smoke.

He stood in this burning cabin as the whole thing swallowed him up, engulfed him.

And then he closed his eyes and let it all take him.

Because he was ready now.

He was ready for Kathryn.

He was ready for David.

He was…

CHAPTER FIFTY

Max was in that room again.

He was in front of the doors. The two doors, both of them with the light shining from them.

Only one of the doors was open now.

The one on the right.

The one where he could see Kathryn.

And where he could see David.

He staggered forward through the clouds beneath his feet. Staggered closer as tears of happiness and joy streamed down his face. Because he was here now. He was here. He'd made it. All this time, and he'd made it, finally.

He'd done what he had to do.

He'd gone back, and he'd stood his ground, and he'd saved Aoife.

Saved Rex.

Shot that glass in and helped them escape.

He got closer and closer to the room with Kathryn and David in. He could hear David's cheeky little laugh as his mother tickled him, played with him. He could see them both giggling, playing, and he wanted that. He wanted to be with them. He wanted to be with them so much.

"I'm coming," he said. "I'm ready now. I'm..."

And that's when the door on the left opened up.

Suddenly. As if a gust of wind had bashed against it.

And inside, beyond, as much as he didn't want to turn to it, as much as he didn't want to look, he saw something that made him stand still.

Made the hairs on his arms stand on end.

Aoife and Seth.

Rex lying dead with his tongue out by their side.

Blood trickling from his body.

Fur ruffled and matted.

And then Seth with Aoife on her knees before him.

Knife to her throat.

Aoife staring back at Max through the door.

And then, the next minute, Seth cut her throat.

Blood everywhere.

And Max froze. Because seeing that, like this, right before him, it scared him.

Because it wasn't how it would happen.

Aoife was strong.

Rex was strong.

They could get away from Seth.

They could defeat him.

Right?

He heard David's laughter again. Saw Kathryn, only she was looking out of the door now. Looking beyond the threshold. Looking at him.

"I'm ready now," Max said. Although there was something else there inside him now, too. An uncertainty. A sense of unease.

Because the images through the other door.

The glimpses he'd got through there.

The glimpses of death.

Of chaos.

Aoife and Rex.

And Seth still standing there, smirking, alive.

"Are you sure you're ready?" Kathryn asked.

And it was torturous, hearing those words. Especially with David being so close. Especially with him being within touching distance.

He'd wanted nothing more than to be reunited with them both for so, so long.

And yet, he knew deep down he couldn't answer Kathryn's question in the way he wanted to.

"Are you sure you're ready?" she repeated.

"I'm not sure I have a choice."

"But you do have a choice," Kathryn said. "You have a choice to fight. You have a choice to make it out of here. You always have a choice."

He stood there, stared into her eyes, and he shook his head.

"But I choose you. I choose David."

"And if you do, can you live with yourself? Or will your choice haunt you?"

He opened his mouth. He wanted to say it was the right choice. He wanted to say he knew what he was doing. He wanted to say it was his only option.

But then he closed his mouth.

He closed his mouth, looked into Kathryn's eyes, and he smiled.

"I'll make it back to you. In time. But I... I know what I need to do now."

Kathryn smiled back at him.

David smiled back at him.

"Then go do it," Kathryn said.

He had one final pull. One final urge yanking him towards going in there. Towards giving up and joining them.

And he resisted that force.

Stood his ground and resisted.
And then he turned around.
He turned to the other door.
To the light.
And then he stepped through it.
His eyes opened.
He saw the flames.
He smelled the smoke.
He felt his body aching everywhere.

And he saw the window, right across the flames, right at the other side of the house.

He knew what he had to do.

CHAPTER FIFTY-ONE

Aoife looked back at the burning cabin and wished there were more she could do.

She stood there. Rex by her side. And she saw it just like she'd seen it with Harry when she was forced to leave him behind in that burning bus. And when the girl died when she was fleeing the plane crash.

She saw the cabin burning, and as much as Max told her to go away, to get to his cabin, something just didn't feel right.

Because she wasn't going to just accept that.

She wasn't going to just give up on him.

"No," she said.

She ran back to the cabin. Looked through the window. The flames looked bad, but not as thick as they were before, somehow.

Maybe she could get back in there.

Maybe she could help him out.

She looked around at the door. There was a metal crowbar across it, which was clearly blocking it. Seth must've put it there.

She grabbed it. Tried to pull it.

But it was wedged across there.

She gritted her teeth. Tightened her palms around it and pulled it again.

And the more she pulled it, as it got hotter and hotter, the more she told herself that this wasn't over.

There was still a chance.

"Come on," she muttered.

She pulled at that crowbar even more. Somewhere behind, she heard Rex growl. And it made the hairs on her arms stand on end.

Because suddenly it dawned on her that Seth was nowhere in sight.

She looked back. Looked at the woods. She swore she saw movement between the trees. Swore she heard laughter. Footsteps. Branches snapping.

She swore she heard all these things, and she knew there was only one solution now.

The house.

Max's house.

He said there were things there that could help her. Supplies there.

Maybe if she got back there in time, she could get back down and save him.

Maybe it wasn't too late.

She turned around and ran back, back up the slope, back towards Max's cabin.

Rex ran alongside her.

She just had to keep going.

She had to get there.

She couldn't give up.

No matter what happened, she was done with giving up on people.

She was done with losing people.

She was going to get Max out of this, and she was going to save him if it was the last thing she did.

She ran further up the slope when she heard a branch snap right behind her.

She stopped. Froze.

Turned around.

Nobody there.

Just a bird, flying past.

The wind blowing against the trees.

A bitter taste filled her mouth. She gritted her teeth. Just her mind. Just her mind playing tricks on her; that's all it was.

She turned back around, and she saw him right away.

Seth stood there.

Machete in his hand.

He looked at her and smiled.

"I don't think so, sis," he said.

CHAPTER FIFTY-TWO

Aoife saw her brother standing before her, machete in hand, and as strong as she was, as assured of her own strength as she may be, she couldn't deny she felt afraid right now.

The winter sun beamed down from above. Aoife's body shook with adrenaline. She could taste blood in the back of her throat and feel a pain on her head where Seth hit her earlier.

But as she stood there, Rex growling by her side, all her focus was on her brother.

His eyes were wide and bloodshot. He looked lost. Lost in that same trance he used to get into so many times when they were younger.

The trance he'd get into when he wanted to torment her.

To punish her.

To make her suffer.

And seeing this look in his eyes as he stood there with this machete, Aoife realised that she'd always been afraid of her brother. That he was the great unknown in her life, even when she'd moved away from him and formed her own life.

She enjoyed the distance. But the fear he was just going to creep up and destroy her life again always haunted her.

Just as he had three years ago when he'd murdered Max's family, and she'd called the police on him.

When the guilt over not reporting him sooner forced her to quit her job in law and pursue something entirely different.

And now again, just as hers and seemingly everyone else's worlds had changed dramatically overnight, here he was.

Machete in hand.

Only this time, she thought he might just be serious.

He might just be for real.

He might just be braced to deliver the most potent form of torture of all.

"Surprised to see you," Seth said. "I locked that cabin door pretty good."

"It's over, Seth."

Seth frowned. "What?"

"It's over. All of it. Whatever fun you're having... it stops. Now. The power's out. And to me it doesn't look like it's going to come back any time soon. So you... you have a chance. A chance to go your own way. A chance to get the hell out of here. A chance you don't deserve. But a chance I'll give you. Because I'm your sister. And despite everything... despite you being a psychopathic nut job. Despite the horrible, horrible things you've done... I won't stand in your way. As long as you get the hell away from here and stay far, far away from me. And far, far away from Max, too. You've caused him enough hurt already. You've caused both of us enough hurt already."

Seth's face turned, just for a moment. She could see his eyes twitching as they darted side to side, really studying her face.

"And why the hell would I walk away?" he asked.

He stepped forward.

"Why, when everything I want to get my revenge on is right here in front of me, would I just turn my back?"

"You expected me not to call the police three years ago? The way you were talking? And with that look in your eyes?"

"We're family. Whether you like it or not. We're family. And family stick together."

"After what you say you did to Dad? You really expect me to believe that?"

She felt pain inside at echoing what Seth had revealed to her. That he'd killed Dad. Everyone thought it was a heart attack. A heart attack right at the top of the stairs.

And yet, it didn't really make sense. Dad was healthy. Especially healthy for a man of his age.

What Seth told her shocked and upset her. But in a way, it didn't surprise her.

Because as unlikely as it seemed, she'd always wondered if there was a possibility.

But no.

She'd never really thought he was capable of that.

Even though she knew everything he was capable of.

And that's where she'd gone wrong.

Seth walked closer to her. She tightened her shaking fists. Rex barked. Behind, she could smell the smoke from the burning cabin. She thought about Max trapped in there. He'd told her to get back to his house. He hadn't died for her to just give up. Especially not to the man who murdered his family.

"Dad wasn't the idol you make him out to be, sis."

"Dad was a good man."

"He was a cheat. A liar. Before you were born, he made Mum's life hell. Sure, you were his little angel. But you were just too ignorant, weren't you? Too ignorant to see how much he mistreated me. Too ignorant to see the monster he turned into after he'd had a drink. Little Aoife never saw any of that, did she? Because she was his sweet girl. His sweet, sweet girl. And she got the easy ride."

Aoife shook her head. She didn't want to hear what Seth was saying. Didn't want to let his words in or let him get to her.

But the more she stood there, the more she remembered.

The shouting.

The smell of booze on Dad's breath.

And the fear in Seth's tearful eyes.

"He wasn't—he wasn't—"

"He wasn't the man you think he was," Seth barked, clearly angry now. "And I thought you'd wisen up in time. I thought you'd grow the fuck up and see through his toxicity eventually. But you didn't. You never did. And when I saw you with Max... the man who took everything away from me... I was turning a corner, Aoife. I was turning a corner, and he arrested Sandy, and she took her life in prison. That broke me. You've no idea how much that broke me."

Once again, Aoife found herself looking into her brother's eyes, and this time, she felt another feeling. She felt sympathy. She actually felt sorry for him.

Because yes, he was a monster.

But she felt guilty. Because he'd been lost as a child.

And he was right about Dad.

It was something she didn't want to face up to.

Something she didn't want to accept because he was always so good to her—and was probably the biggest influence on her entire life.

But he wasn't good with Seth.

For whatever reason, he wasn't good with him.

But then, in an instant, Seth wiped his tearful eyes.

He took a deep breath.

His nostrils twitched.

"But you wouldn't understand," he said. "Because you're just like him. His sweet little princess."

He pulled back the machete.

Went to swing it at Aoife.

That's when she heard the voice.

"Stop."

Seth froze.

Everything froze.

She looked around, heart racing, and saw the man emerging from the smoke-filled background.

His clothes were tattered.

He was covered in sweat.

He had cuts, bruises, and burns everywhere.

But it was him.

Max.

Max was here.

Max was alive.

"Put down the machete," he said. Hunting rifle in hand. Pointed right at Seth. "Right this fucking instant."

CHAPTER FIFTY-THREE

Max saw Seth in the distance, machete hovering before Aoife, and he felt nothing but a deep, burning anger and rage right inside.

He felt exhausted. His whole body was sore. The bandage he'd wrapped around his side, where he'd been stabbed, had been burned at and come loose. His legs shook. His lungs felt charred from all the smoke inhalation. He wasn't sure how much energy he had left in his system. How much fuel he had left in the tank.

But he'd made it this far. And for a reason.

He'd made it this far because he'd not gone through that door to Kathryn and to David.

He'd made it this far because he knew, deep down, his work wasn't done.

He'd made it this far because he couldn't let Aoife die at the hands of her psychopathic brother, regardless of whether she'd had a chance at stopping his family dying or not, three years ago.

Seth stopped. He lowered his machete. Both he and Aoife stared over at him. Rex sat by Aoife's side, clearly torn between wanting to protect her and defend her and wagging his tail at seeing Max again.

"Well," Seth said. "Max. I did not expect you to emerge from the flames. Looking a little worse for wear, though, brother, I must say."

Max clutched the rifle with his shaking fingers. Pointed right at Seth. He wasn't here to talk. He wasn't here for any messing around at all.

He was here to get his revenge against Seth, once and for all.

And to stop him killing Aoife and Rex in the process.

"Put the machete down," Max said.

Seth smiled. "I always knew you were a tough cookie. But you're an even tougher cookie than I—"

Max fired a bullet, which ricocheted just past Seth.

So close to Seth he actually saw his hair flutter in the breeze of the passing bullet.

"I'm not here to listen to your bullshit. Not a word of it. Put the machete down. And get on your knees. Right this second."

Seth stood there, prone, stationary.

His eyes darted from Max to Aoife, his sister, who stared back at Max, wide-eyed.

"Machete down. And on your knees. Now."

Seth shook his head.

He lowered the machete to his side.

"That's the problem, Max. I won't kneel to you. I won't ever kneel to you. Because I don't kneel to anyone."

Max saw him standing there. Saw that smug smirk on his face.

And he knew there was no holding back anymore.

He pulled the trigger.

Fired right at Seth's left kneecap.

Seth let out a yelp.

Fell to the ground.

Blood spurting out from that left knee.

He could hear Seth's pain as he clutched his leg.

Hear him wailing. Crying.

And yet, as he stepped closer to him, with no concept of his surroundings anymore, with no idea of anything but what was right before him, he found himself revelling in Seth's pain.

"Max," Aoife said.

But he ignored her.

He pushed past her.

He stood over Seth, who sat there, bleeding out on the icy ground.

And he wanted to look into his terrified eyes.

He wanted to see his pain.

But when Seth looked up at him, Max saw something else, there in his gaze.

Seth was still smirking.

He was still laughing.

"Three years," he said. "Three years and still I'm living rent-free in your head. And that's torture enough for me. That's satisfaction enough for me. And if this is my moment, if this is my time... at least I'll know I drove you to this. At least I'll know it was *me* who broke you. Just like you broke me. And at least I'll know it'll be me you think of when you go to sleep at night."

He heard Seth's words; he heard no remorse, nothing of the kind.

And it just riled him up even more.

He pulled back his rifle and swung it across Seth's face.

He heard the sound of the man's teeth cracking as the metal smacked against it.

He heard Seth's pained grunt and watched blood splatter from his mouth.

He saw him lying there on the ground, and then he heard something else.

"Don't do it, Max," Aoife said. "Don't do it. Don't do what he wants you to do. Be better than him."

He heard Aoife's words. And he wanted to honour them. He wanted to hold off. He wanted to resist.

But the pain of losing Kathryn.

Of losing David.

It was still just as strong today as it was back that day three years ago.

"It won't help you," Kathryn said. "It won't help anything."

He saw Seth staring up at him. His face was bruised and bloodied. He looked broken. Defeated.

But still, he had that smirk on his face.

That smile.

"Go on," he spat. "He peed himself, you know? Little David. He peed himself when I was holding the blade to his neck. I felt it, trickling right down his leg. Right down."

And then Max fired another bullet, this one in Seth's shoulder.

Another grunt from Seth.

Another yelp of agony.

But more than anything… that smirk was still there.

He looked down at Seth. Broken. Bleeding.

He looked down at him, and he felt there was only one option here.

There was only one thing he could do.

He felt it all, and then he lifted his rifle.

Pointed it at Seth's head.

"You don't say his name."

"David? He was so scared. So afraid. He just wanted you to help him. And you failed him."

Max tightened his grip on the trigger.

"Shut up."

Seth laughed. In agony but laughing. "And Kathryn, too. Sweet, sweet Kathryn. I had plans for her, you know? It's a shame you got here when you did. Because I was really, really looking forward to seeing what she looked like a little more… well. Intimately. Same with David, too, actually."

Max tightened the trigger even more.

Heart racing.

Chest tight.

"Don't do it," Aoife whispered. "Max, don't do this. Don't listen to him. Don't do what he wants you to do."

He looked into Seth's eyes.

Looked into Seth's smirking gaze.

And he felt like this was all on rails.

He felt like he didn't have a choice.

"Go on. Or are you a coward? Are you going to hesitate again? Just like you did back then?"

Max stood his ground.

He pointed that rifle.

Just a millimetre from pulling that trigger and finishing him, once and for all.

"Don't, Max," Aoife said. "You don't want this on your conscience. Don't do it."

He looked down at Seth, and he felt a certainty about what he had to do.

And then he heard a voice in his head.

Kathryn's voice.

No.

He lowered the rifle.

He threw it to the ground.

And he looked right into Seth's eyes.

"You've tortured me for years. But you won't make me do this. I won't give you what you want."

For just an instant, he saw the smug smirk drift from Seth's face.

Saw the smile drop.

Saw his eyes widen.

Like he hadn't got what he wanted.

And then Max turned around to Aoife.

To Rex.

He staggered towards them both.

Saw Aoife looking at him with wide eyes.

"You did the right thing," she said, nodding.

Then she walked past him.

Walked over towards Seth.

Max stood there. Facing the other way. Facing the rising smoke. Facing the flames emerging from the cabin.

And as he stood there, he knew he couldn't look back.

He didn't want to look Seth in the eyes again.

He wanted this to be his closure.

He wanted this to be the end of—

He heard a blast.

He looked around.

Aoife stood over Seth.

She had Max's rifle in hand.

She was pointing it at her brother.

Her brother, who was missing half of his face.

Whose brains spilled out from his cracked half skull.

"Max might be able to walk away," she said. "But I can't. This was for Dad."

And then she dropped the rifle to the ground, and Seth fell to his side right before her.

Max looked at Aoife.

Looked at her as she stared down at her brother's corpse, twitching away.

He looked at Seth lying there, dead. The threat eliminated.

He looked, and he saw Aoife turn around.

Saw her look at him. A distance to her eyes.

"You didn't have to do what he wanted you to do," she said. "But... but I did. I did."

He stared at her as she stood there, pale, haunted like she'd seen a ghost.

And inside, he felt peace.

He felt like it was over.

And yet, at the same time, he felt sad.

For Aoife.
That she was living with this now.
She walked away from Seth's twitching body.
Walked away and towards Max. Towards Rex.
Seth stared up through his one eye.
He wasn't smirking anymore.

CHAPTER FIFTY-FOUR

"Hold still."

"I'm holding still."

"Well, hold stiller."

"I can do this myself."

"No," Aoife said. "You're hurt. Bad. Your hands are shaky. You can't do it yourself. You need to trust me."

Max went to argue with Aoife. But in the end, he closed his mouth, and he sighed. She was right. His hands were shaky. He felt battered and bruised like he'd been through a right beating. His lungs were hoarse, and he felt exhausted.

He knew he shouldn't even be here. He was lucky to be alive.

And he had to be grateful for the fact he *was* still here. That was a miracle in itself.

But right now, he had to trust in Aoife.

Even though he was worried about her.

They were back at his house. They'd both walked back up here with Rex. Neither of them said much on the walk back. Barely exchanged a word, in fact.

There was so much Max wanted to say. Because he'd waited

for an opportunity to get his revenge on Seth for so long, and then he'd been denied it.

And yet, strangely, he felt better for *not* killing Seth.

He felt better for it because he knew that killing Seth would've been what Seth wanted.

It would've elevated Seth in his own mind.

And that's not the kind of victory he wanted to grant Seth.

But then he looked at Aoife, and he saw the haunted look on her pale face. She looked like she'd aged in the space of a day. He supposed they all had, in a way.

But she'd just killed her brother.

She'd just shot and killed her own brother.

And it scared Max. Because if this was the actions of one ordinary girl on day one of the blackout, then who knows what other mini battles the rest of the country—or even the world, if that's how big this was—were engaged in?

Who knew just how much society had slipped already?

And would it ever fix itself?

How *could* it fix itself when so much trauma had been experienced and suffered in the first few hours?

But now, he sat here on his sofa and watched as Aoife stitched him up with her shaking hands. He didn't trust her, especially with his own medical experience. Doctors always made the worst patients, after all.

But he knew he had to sit back. And he had to accept the help he needed right now.

Besides. It would help Aoife to get her mind off what she'd done.

He hated Seth. He despised him for what he'd done.

And he felt an element of animosity towards Aoife, too. Because she could've stopped her brother doing what he'd done. She could've acted sooner.

But then so could he.

So could everyone.

Hindsight was a wonderful thing.

"Are you okay?" he asked, wincing as the needle pierced his flesh.

"I'm fine," Aoife said.

"I just... With what happened. I figured I'd check—"

"I don't want to talk about it. It's done. I'm fine. Okay?"

He heard Aoife's snappy voice. Saw the way she glared at him, pale, exhausted, big bags under her eyes. And he knew she was suffering. He knew she was in pain. He knew this was going to be difficult for her. A struggle for her.

And as much as he felt uncomfortable opening up himself, as much as he found it difficult bonding and attaching with other people... he knew Aoife was going to need to talk to someone at some stage.

"Just know I'm here," he said. "When you need me."

She looked at him. Looked at him like she was going to say something else.

And then she nodded. Half-smiled.

She would talk.

In her own time, she would talk.

Just not yet.

"Well," she said. "I think I'm done."

Max investigated his stitches. "Not done a bad job, actually."

"Told you that you could trust me."

Max grunted. "We'll get there."

He stood up. Walked over towards the door of the house.

"You sure you should be walking just yet?"

"Probably not," Max said, wincing a little. But then he stood at the door and stared outside. At the trees. At the grass. At the sunlight.

Aoife walked up to his side, and Rex joined them both.

And the three of them just stood there for a while. Stood there, staring out into the unknown.

But there was a question coming that Max *knew* was coming.

A question he'd been trying to hide from.

But a question he couldn't run away from.

"You... you can stay here. If you want."

Aoife looked around at him. Narrowed her eyes.

"I'm just saying. There's... there's three bedrooms. You can take one of them. If you want to, anyway. Until... well. Let's just see how things go, okay?"

Aoife looked right into his eyes. And for a moment, he thought she was going to reject him. He thought she was going to tell him she wasn't staying here. She was moving on.

But then she smiled.

"Thank you," she said. "I appreciate that."

Max nodded, his walls erecting again instantly. "You'll have to pull your weight, though. Hunting. Gathering wood. Cooking. Those kinds of things. That's your rent."

Aoife smiled. "Don't worry. I know a thing or two about survival."

"Good," Max said. "Because you're gonna need to know it."

He stood there, by Aoife's side.

Rex between them.

Stared out at the bright January sun.

"Here's to a new year," Aoife said.

Max took a deep breath.

He saw those two doors in his mind.

The one he'd gone through.

And the one with Kathryn and David inside.

The one that was shut—for now.

He swallowed a lump in his throat, and he tightened his fists.

"Here's to a new world," he said.

* * *

MAX HAD A FEELING this was going to be bad for the long haul.

He had a feeling so many things were going to change, for good.

He knew he was going to have to be resourceful.

He knew he was going to have to dig as deep as he possibly could if he wanted to survive.

But he still had no idea just how momentous the events of New Year's Eve were going to be.

He had no idea just how much his life was going to change.

Nobody did.

But they were about to find out.

Everyone was about to find out.

END OF BOOK 1

Escape the Darkness, the second book in the Survive the Darkness series, is now available on Amazon.

If you want to be notified when Ryan Casey's next novel is released—and receive an exclusive post apocalyptic novel totally free—sign up for the author newsletter: ryancaseybooks.com/fanclub

Printed in Great Britain
by Amazon